WOMEN

ARE

WONDEROUS

ERATH McKIAH

Women

are

Wonderous

Dr Erath McKiah

All individual characters in this book are

fictionalized composites of multiple

real historical people,

some still in sunlight,

most now in shadow.

Eiryanna l

During his High School years in New Haven, Connecticut, Gareth Emeralde played halfback in football. His best buddy Erin, whom he idolized, was the quarterback. In their senior year, their team won the State Championship. Gareth and Erin had for several years been engaged in a lively debate as to what course a young man's life should take. They both agreed on most items and only debated the finer points. New Haven was boring. Getting married, settling down, and having children was a trap. Life should be an ongoing adventure full of freedom, conquest, and glorious victory. The military was where all the adventure was to be found, but what branch? Boats were too confining, and the infantry too demeaning.

They both agreed that the Cavalry, with all the dignity of a robust stallion, was the way to go. The history and tactics of Cavalry down through the ages became an obsessive discussion between the two. Was it Genghis Khan's Mongols, or were the Comanche the best Cavalry of all time? They debated why Napoleon's Marshall Ney's Cavalry had been defeated by the British Squares at Waterloo. What mistakes did General Custer make at Little Big Horn?

During the summer of their eighteenth year, with the fire of youth aglow, Gareth and Erin became intrigued by stories of the Rough Riders Brigade. Early one summer morning, Gareth and Erin went downtown as a team and enlisted in the Army, joining the Rough Riders Brigade. The Cavalry was a young man's dream come true. They trained together on valiant steeds in the rugged hills of North Dakota under the heroic leadership of Teddy Roosevelt

Roosevelt was a titan with the nobility of those who dwelt on Olympus. He had a father's instructive instinct that drove him to instill in his troops the Platonic virtues of knowledge, courage, and self-discipline. He was determined to build each man, in his thousand-plus brigade, into the finest cavalry soldier possible. After training in North Dakota, Roosevelt led his troops down into the hellish swamps of the Everglades of South Florida. In the Everglades, they were trained to overcome any obstacle on horseback, no matter how difficult. With the outbreak of war with Spain in late April, Gareth and Erin knew that this was their call to adventure.

They arrived in Cuba only to find themselves without their gallant steeds. Due to the laziness of some desk jockey in Washington, who had failed to fill out the proper paperwork, their horses had been left stranded in Florida. Only Roosevelt had his mount because he had insisted it travel with him on the troop transport ship. As highly trained cavalry soldiers, they were relegated to slopping through the mud in ill-fitting, water-logged Army boots.

Due to Roosevelt's determined acquisition, the Rough Riders carried the Model 1896 Springfield Armory 30 caliber smokeless cartridge bolt-action carbine, affectionately known as the 'Krag.' The Krag was a vast improvement over the old 1873 45-caliber black powder trapdoor rifle issued to most American soldiers in this expedition.

However, Roosevelt knew that the Spanish soldiers carried the Model 1893 Mauser 53 caliber (7.65mm) smokeless cartridge carbine, the best war rifle of the era. The Mauser had a greater muzzle velocity and hurled a slug almost twice the width of the Krag slug. These features gave the Mauser a much greater stopping power than the Krag. The Mauser had a charger loaded 5-shot magazine that allowed faster feeding of the cartridges into the chamber. The top benefit of the Mauser was that it had the best long-range accuracy of any rifle on the field of combat. Roosevelt had read everything he could get his hands on about the 1893 Mauser. Roosevelt feared that weapon.

The morning of July 1, 1898, was a date Gareth often prayed to forget. He and his buddy Erin found themselves encamped in a hot, steamy jungle on the southern shores of Cuba. They were trapped at the bottom of two hills, pinned down by Spanish artillery and rifle fire. Shells were exploding all around them, and men were dying everywhere. The Spanish Soldiers were dug in on the ridges of the two hills above them, firing down on the Americans with their deadly accurate Mausers. The Rough Riders were struggling to find any cover possible. The situation continued to deteriorate and grow more hopeless by the hour.

The American Commanders, finding themselves in an unwinnable position, had ordered their troops to hunker down. The feckless Army leaders were unwilling to charge the hills, fearing massive troop losses and inevitable defeat. But Teddy Roosevelt, a brilliant military tactician, seeing first-hand the deadly effects of the Mauser, considered taking matters into his own hands. If he had to spit Commodore Dewey himself in the eye and face court-marshal, he was not going to let his coveted Trojan warriors perish in the valley of the shadow.

While the Officers debated, a determined Roosevelt decided not to wait for orders but to charge Kettle Hill. Mounting his steed, he gathered his valiant Rough Riders with the call of a bugle. Despite the incoming artillery blasts and the withering Spanish rifle volleys, the Rough Riders charged resolutely up Kettle Hill with Roosevelt in the lead. The sweat-soaked soldiers' fear gave way to unbridled courage as they plowed uphill through the ushes and brambles. Brave men were falling all around them, but stubbornly, ье Rough Riders began to charge even faster and with greater boldness.

Roosevelt and his Rough Riders, in glorious triumph, took Kettle Hill. They then turned and charged up San Juan Hill. As soon as the Rough Riders topped San Juan Hill, the Spanish soldiers began to flee in the rection of Santiago. Caught up in the explosive adrenaline-filled high of ctory, the Rough Riders, as one man, let out a spontaneous thundering rebel ll. All of the bitter struggles of the day vanished into the pure elation of a oble conquest decisively won.

Out of the corner of his eye, Gareth caught the glint of a fleeing panish soldier's rifle turning toward him. Gareth quickly pivoted. The ldier's Mauser fired. Gareth's return shot knocked the Spanish soldier own. The next instant, Gareth reflexly twisted to look back towards his ompatriot. To his absolute horror, he saw Erin fall to the ground. The slug d struck Erin in the chest. Erin, the only friend he had ever known, died ere in his blood-soaked arms. In that agonizing moment of utter despair, all e glory of war faded into the hollow bitterness of death. Somewhere in the rk canyons of that cataclysmic event, all of Gareth's ill-conceived notions of eedom and adventure perished as well.

Gareth returned home to New Haven, a war hero with malaria and a ounded heart. He initially boarded at a place called the Century House while recovered from malaria. In time, he got a job no one else wanted, changing tomobile tires at a local garage. Gareth worked hard at his new job and came very proficient at changing tires. Gareth spent a lot of time at the rary on Elm Street, reading everything he could find about automobile tires.

One day, upon returning home exhausted from work, he met a beautiful young High School girl. Briana was on her knees with a bucket and brush scrubbing the floor. Briana was the daughter of the woman who owned the boarding house. Over the next year or so, they would spontaneously engage long conversations about anything and everything. Just having someone to ta to eased the pain hidden deep in Gareth's heart. Briana and Gareth accidentally fell in love.

Gareth started a tire business in New Haven that eventually became very successful. During their engagement, Gareth built a marvelous three-sto house on Pine Street, especially for his sweetheart, Briana. Gareth and Briana were married in St Patrick's Cathedral. The reception was a lavish event with all the old Irish Families in attendance.

In the course of time, Mr and Mrs Emeralde were blessed with seven high-energy children. They drove new Lincoln automobiles, dressed well, and went to all the best restaurants in town. The family took marvelous vacations and spent almost the entire month of August in a quaint white cottage at Seabluff Beach.

On October 29, 1929, Eiryanna Emeralde, Gareth's fourth child, wa fourteen years old and in the seventh grade. Eiryanna was walking home fron school that afternoon and, as usual, met her father on the sidewalk, walking th other way. Gareth, as always, was dressed in a well-tailored black suit with a gold watch in the vest pocket. He was holding a black silver-tipped cane, sporting a black bowler hat, and wearing shiny black wingtip oxford dress sho

Their conversation began as usual in the same polite yet superficial manner. "Good afternoon, Eiryanna. How are you doing," he said in a distar fashion. Eiryanna answered in a scripted, "Wonderful Father, how are you doing." This particular afternoon, Gareth was very troubled. Noticing his wrinkled brow, she continued, "You just looked so worried it made me very concerned." Her question caused a door to open inside Gareth's mind, prompting him to reply. "I know you have heard me talk about the stock market many times in the past and how it affects the economy. Well, the stock values have continued to fall again today and some people think that things are going to get much worse before things get any better! But don't you worry, people will always need new tires for their automobiles, so my business is very safe. I will see you at home in just a little while." They gave each other a polite hug and continued on their separate ways.

As the stock market crash continued to evolve, everything began to change for the worse. New Haven slowly degenerated in appearance from a prosperous sanctum into that of a rundown tenement in a darker corner of Purgatory. The yards became overgrown and stuffed rusting trash cans lined the curbs. The cars on the road, now unwashed, became fewer and fewer as people could no longer afford gasoline.

Eireyanna's family began to eat hamburger instead of steak. The maid who cleaned the house disappeared without notice. Their industrious and supportive mother, Briana, began to teach all the children how to do the dishes, scrub the kitchen floor, and clean their own rooms. With great detail, Briana showed the children how to iron their Catholic School Uniforms and sew on a button. The Lincoln vanished, and a rusty used Ford replaced it in the garage.

One dark, cold, windy February morning, a powerful storm deposited a layer of sleet over the entire town. With the progression of the day, the melting sleet refroze as the bitter cold of the winter storm firmed its iron grip on New

Haven. Tree branches of great size began to fall, and soon, the whole town was without power. Briana calmed the children's fears as they lit the two fireplaces and the well-positioned oil lamps retained for such emergencies. All the children gathered in the spacious living room and began to sing songs and play joyful board games.

Suddenly, the front door burst open and then slammed shut. A very sullen, angry version of their father appeared in the hush-quiet of the living room. He barked out harsh commands, sending the children to their bedrooms not to reappear until he had finished his meeting with their mother. From the study, they could hear the loud proclamations of their father and the continuous weeping of their sweet mother. In the following weeks, they learned that their father had lost his once profitable business of twenty-six years and had been forced into something called bankruptcy.

Briana watched as the family's finances went down and down. She began fearing that they would not be able to pay the taxes and would lose their house. She rented the downstairs basement to a Greek immigrant widow, but that only covered a portion of the monthly bills. Reluctantly Briana got out her bucket and brush. She began going door to door, finding work scrubbing floors. In the following years, Briana helped put six of her seven children through college during the depression, scrubbing floors on her hands and knees.

Genetics 1

Gregor Mendel was a Moravian monk who had an intense interest in garden plants. Mendel observed that the pea plants in his garden had different lower colors, and he was determined to discover the cause. He reasoned that the plants must maintain and transmit the 'code' for the appearance of the color trait. Mendel called these coding instructions 'elemente.' Mendel's elemente are now known as genes. Mendel postulated that in reproduction, the male flower transmitted one elemente and the female flower transmitted a different elemente. These elemente were then combined in the offspring to produce the color observed.

In 1866, Mendel published a scientific paper titled 'Experiments on Plant Hybrids.' This study detailed his findings ascertained during his cross-breeding experiments involving garden peas. This paper and its findings went largely unnoticed during his lifetime and were not rediscovered until the turn of the twentieth century.

At the age of thirty-eight, Nettie Stephens, a Vermont native, received her Bachelor's Degree from what was to become Stanford University in California. Stephens went on to attend Bryn Mawr College in Philadelphia, where she became a pioneer in genetic research. While at Bryn Mawr, Stephens earned her Master's Degree and Ph.D. in Science. Stephen's passion was to discover what biological force determined the sex of organisms.

In 1905, Nettie Stephens, PhD, published a paper entitled "Studies in Spermatogenesis." This publication asserted that an organism's sex is determined by hereditary traits passed down through the chromosomes. Further, the paper concluded that females of the species are born with a pair of XX sex chromosomes, and males are born with XY sex chromosomes. This paper also concluded that in the male of the species, the X sex chromosome comes from the mother, and the Y sex chromosome comes from the father. In that same year, Thomas H. Morgan, Ph.D., and Edmund Wilson, Ph.D., two of Stephens's instructors, had arrived at the same findings as Stephens on chromosomal sex determination.

In 1912, at fifty years of age, Nettie Stephens, Ph.D., died of breast cancer, and the world lost one of its finest minds. In 1933, Thomas H. Morgan Ph.D., Stephens's mentor at Bryn Mawr, was awarded the Nobel Prize in Medicine for his discoveries concerning the sex chromosomal role in heredity. Nettie Stephens never received due credit for her groundbreaking discoveries (1), (2), (3).

Breast Cancer

Globally, breast cancer causes at least one million deaths per year in women. Breast cancer is most likely to affect women after their fiftieth year. On average, half of all breast cancers occur in women with no specific risk factors other than age. It is important to note that most breast lumps (tumors) are benign (non-cancerous) and do not spread beyond the breast tissue. For the most part, these tumors are not life-threatening. However, some types of benign breast tumors can increase the risk of getting malignant breast cancer.

Breast cancer occurs when cells in the breast tissue mutate and grow out of control, creating a mass of tissue (tumor). This mutated tissue can metastasize (invade) the tissue surrounding the breast. These metastatic cancer cells can then travel either by the lymphatic system or by the bloodstream into distant parts of the body, forming new tissue tumors. Breast cancer designations are based upon the nature of the tissue of origin. Most

east cancers are derived from the epithelial cells that line the internal tissue of
e breast and are, therefore, labeled as carcinomas.

The most common breast cancers, such as ductal carcinoma in situ and
vasive carcinoma, are labeled as adenocarcinomas since they start in the milk-
oducing ducts and glands. Ductal carcinoma in situ (original place) is
recancerous) because the cells have not spread beyond the ducts.
filtrating (invasive) ductal carcinoma begins in the milk ducts, then breaks
rough the duct wall and spreads into the surrounding tissue. This is the most
mmon type, representing about eighty percent of all breast cancers.
filtrating (invasive) lobular (milk-producing glands) carcinoma accounts for
out ten percent of breast cancers.

Tripple-negative breast cancer (TNBC) is one of the most challenging
pes because it lacks three of the markers needed for diagnosis; therefore, its
ognosis and treatment remain difficult. Inflammatory breast cancer is a rare
d aggressive type hallmarked by redness, swelling, pitting, and dimpling of the
east skin. It is caused by obstructive cancer cells in the lymph vessels of the
in. Paget's disease affects the skin of the nipple and the areola. (4).

Eiryanna II

The Local hardware store had survived the stock market crash and its
ner was a good friend of Gareth Emeralde. Knowing Gareth's situation, he
fered him an hourly job at the hardware store. Gareth thanked him
spectively but refused the job. Gareth considered himself a businessman, a
ss above those who earned their living by the sweat of their brows and the toil
their soiled hands. Eventually, Gareth had a head-on confrontation with the
n in the mirror. He, reluctantly and out of sheer necessity, began to help his

father, Thomas, a designer of mill machinery, repair that machinery in a small workshop behind the Pine Street home.

Eiryanna continued to greet her father every afternoon on her walk hom from school. One afternoon, many months after his bankruptcy, Gareth was his usual walk. On this day, he was wearing an old work coat, scuffed work boots, and his hands were stained with machine oil. He would normally say, "Good afternoon, Eiryanna. How are you doing." Eiryanna would then customarily respond, "Wonderful Father, how are you doing." On this occasion, however, Eiryanna could feel her father's sorrow and, without a wor simply clasped his hand, turned, and began to walk with him. Tears of empath streamed down her cheeks as they walked in silence together. When she look up, she saw one brave tear on the old warrior's furrowed cheek.

One feature of the house on Pine Street was a small garden room with three sides full of windows. Early in their marriage, Briana and Gareth plant an extensive rose garden immediately outside the garden room. Throughout their long marriage, they sequestered time to spend together at least two or three times a week. After the children had been fed, they would sit at a small table in the garden room and share dinner. Their after-dinner discussions we relaxed and full of the events of the day, the issues of the children, and their hopes and dreams for the future. In the dark days and years after the crash, these dinners and conversations took on a whole new perspective and became filled with prayer. This time together preserved their marriage and their famil a time when marriages and families were disintegrating all around them.

Genetics II

The sex of a creature is determined by its specific chromosomal content at conception. An embryo with two X sex chromosomes will become a female, while an embryo with an X-Y combination results in a male. The Y sex chromosome, from the male, contains between 70 to 200 genes. The X sex chromosome is considerably larger than the Y sex chromosome, containing between 900 to 1400 genes. Of the two X sex chromosomes that define the female, one copy originates from the mother, and the other copy originates from the father.

It had been long postulated, but never proven, that one of the X sex chromosomes in the female was functionally inactivated or 'silent.' Recent research, however, has revealed that a wide variance exists as to which genes (if any) become inactivated and which genes remain active on the (not so) silent X sex chromosome. One study showed that as many as 340 genes on the supposedly silent female X sex chromosomes remained active / non-silent. The reality of at least partial activation of the 'silent' female X sex chromosome demonstrates that females, as contrasted to males, are mosaics of both X cell populations (the X from the father and the X from the mother). In comparing the number of genes being expressed, the female XX sex chromosome pair has at least one hundred and perhaps as many as a <u>thousand</u> more genes being expressed in the cell than the male XY sex chromosome pair.

Research into this quandary is ongoing. This combination of both X sex chromosomes is just beginning to be understood in biological science and social constructs. One thing is certain: Women have a much greater genetic diversity than men because they are a mosaic of the mother's X and the father's X chromosome. Due to this double X gene pair, women also possess vastly more genetic expression than men. This greater genetic diversity and greater genetic expression can be thought of as stronger genetic gravity.

This greater genetic gravity of females can be seen in the female's life-bringer role through the preservation of the species by having children. Women's exponentially expanded genetic gravity makes them vastly superior to men in all the elements that make life more beautiful, profoundly meaningful, and joyfully worth living. Evidence of this gravity can be seen in their abounding empathy which results in such realities as their attention to aging parents and their tender care for infants.

Is all of this genetic complexity accidental, or is it the evidence of a grand design? Assuming the design hypothesis to be correct, one can make the analogy that men are designed to be like dump trucks and women are designed to be like sports cars. A thinking individual would never use a dump truck to race at Le-mans, nor would they use a sports car to haul gravel. (5), (6), (7), (8), (9).

Regan I

The robust outburst of Fall arbor color invigorated Rhyland Golden as he walked, at a brisk pace, to work early at 6 am. Rhyland and his wife Rose had been blessed with six marvelous children. Rhyland's oldest girl, Marin, had just begun college at the University of Connecticut in Mansfield with a determined goal of becoming a nurse. Fiona, his teenage comedian who was always ready with a tart quip, was in her last year in High School. Deirdre wanted to be a

un. Muriel loved to paint with oils. Ailbhe was going to be on Broadway and
ne day be famous beyond belief. His youngest, Regan, was a happy, robust
oy. Regan loved to play catch with his brand-new glove that he had recently
gotten from his Dad on his tenth birthday. Rhyland considered himself to be a
appy homebody. He treasured spending time with his beautiful redheaded
wife and frolicking children.

Ryland Golden was a stockbroker and a leading citizen in New Haven.
Greatly respected by all because he had made many a man in that municipality
very wealthy. As he walked to work, Ryland was full of bright hopes for the
future. A month prior, he had purchased an acre of land on a prestigious hilltop
elevated above the town. In his mind, he was busy planning every detail of the
mansion he would build on that hilltop. Upon entering the office, as was his
habit, he corrected the date display to read Tuesday, October 29, 1929. He
then went straight to work, getting caught up on all the purchases he had made
during yesterday's Monday downturn.

Rhyland was very comfortable with the cyclic nature of the market. He
saw a market downturn as an opportunity to purchase discount stocks that he
could quickly sell for a profit when the market was on the up-swing. Ryland did a
good bit of buying that morning. By afternoon, he began to realize that
something was going terribly awry. He made a phone call to a trusted colleague
in New York City. His friend told him, in a voice trembling with fear, to freeze
all of his accounts, close his office immediately, and take all his money out of the
bank today.

Rhyland made a superficial excuse to send his staff home early for the
day. After they had exited, he flipped the door sign to closed and put a
padlock on the outside of his office door. At the bank, which already had a line

out the door, he withdrew all but twenty dollars from his accounts. He proceeded to the grocery store and purchased a month's worth of canned goods from already thinning shelves. People that had greeted him with a smile in the past were now sullen and looked at him with barely concealed contempt.

Rhyland drove to his house, parked the Lincoln in the garage, and went in to inform his wife of the evolving market crash. After a brief conversation, they both sat in silence and listened to the news on the radio with all the children present. Upon listening to the radio for about half an hour, he turned it off. He then proceeded to answer the children's questions with positive, assuring responses as best he could to allay their fears. That evening the family sat through a very silent supper in which the food was barely touched. As the sun began to set, the children were sent to bed early amidst the gathering gloom.

In the coming weeks and months, the situation in town and in the nation continued to go from bad to worse. Longstanding businesses began to close, and long lines of visibly angry, out of work, men could be seen outside soup kitchens. The neighborhoods had become run down with unmowed lawns and overflowing rusted trash cans at the curb. Rhyland intentionally dressed in shabby work clothes and switched vehicles to the old Model T he had driven in his college days. The grocery store shelves were now stripped of food, and all the banks had padlocks on their doors.

In the newspapers he began to read about stockbrokers who had committed suicide and some who had been found in alleys dead, full of bullet holes. One day, as he drove by his old office, he saw that the windows had all been smashed out, and the door had been ripped off its hinges. Rhyland came to the hard realization that at some point, in the not-too-distant future, he would have to find some sort of work in another state.

Rhyland started to notice, again and again, a black Cadillac with New

ork plates in his rearview mirror. A chill went down his spine as he realized he

as being followed. For the first time in his civilian life, Rhyland began carrying

s Colt 45 single-action army pistol. In 1904, during his army training at the

avalry outpost outside Marfa, Texas, he had won several marksmanship

vards with that pistol. He served in the Cavalry during peacetime and had

pt the gun only as a souvenir.

One afternoon, as he drove home from town, a black Cadilac came up

hind him at high speed and rammed his bumper. Speeding up, fear

erwhelmed him, and he began to shake. Very darkly, he knew what he had to

and that there would be no second-place award in this contest. At high

eed, he turned his jittery Model T down a dirt road that was familiar to him.

he road went north from town into the woods and ended several miles away in

acant cul-de-sac. When he got to the cul-de-sac, he whipped his vehicle

ound and finalized the chase with his Model T facing the opposing Cadilac.

ith ice water running through his veins, Rhyland stepped out of his car. He

lked to its front with his 45 tucked in his belt concealed behind his coat flap.

wo large, barrel-chested men dressed in black suits slowly emerged from the

adilac. They stood silently with evil, confident grins eight feet from where he

od, their hands on their holstered pistols.

With calm determination, Rhyland quickly drew his Colt 45 Revolver and,

ercising great precision, shot each man in the heart. He then dragged the

sest man by the back of his coat several feet away from the Cadillac. He

sitioned him with his feet pointing toward the other man who lay beside the

od-splattered Cadilac. He shot each man with the other's revolver two times

he chest. He then shot each of their pistols once into the woods. He wiped both of their revolvers with his handkerchief. Placing each man's gun into their own grip, he let their arms fall at their side on the gravel road. He resolutely drove out of the cul-de-sac, stopped, and obliterated his tire tracks with a dea tree branch.

As Rhyland began his drive home, a surge of exhilaration exploded from his core due to the realization that he had just escaped certain death. Gradually, the exhilaration faded, and the hard reality of the consequences began to settle in. As a long-time crime novel enthusiast, he knew there was n such thing as the perfect crime. Someone in town must have witnessed the chase. If the authorities bothered to dig out the bullets from the deceased, th would soon realize that there was a third party involved. The organization tha had sent out the first two killers would not be fooled. In very short order, more efficient killers would arrive, and this time by the cover of darkness. His belov family would then certainly be in harm's way. Deep gloom enveloped his soul a he came to a very painful realization. The only solution available to escape hi deadly predicament was to very quickly vanish without a trace.

Upon arriving at his house, he parked the Model T in the driveway. H greeted his wife, Rose, without his usual bright smile, then went to his room an packed a duffle bag. He gathered all the cash he had left in the world and too a roll twenty-dollar bills out for himself. He placed a much larger roll of bills in his wife's top dresser drawer. By that time, dinner was ready, and he went downstairs to share what he knew would be his last meal with his beloved famil

Rhyland began the meal with a prayer. After dinner, he gathered his family into the living room and turned on the radio show 'Suspense.' Once th children had become enthralled in the drama, Rose and he went out into the garage and sat in the Lincoln. Rhyland explained to Rose what had transpire in the chase and at the Cul-de-sac. After her uncontrolled sobbing abated slightly, he relayed to Rose the soon-to-be overwhelming danger that awaited their family. He explained with great pain why his only option was to leave town immediately.

After Rose had regained a measure of self-control, she and Rhyland returned to the living room, where the episode of 'Suspense' was winding to a close. Rhyland sat the children down at the dinner table and told them that he had to go to Florida on a business trip but that he would be back soon. Between the sobbing and the pleadings of "Oh, Pappa, please don't go," utter sadness enveloped his soul.

Rhyland assumed that both of his automobiles were known by site. He also realized that all the usual transportation hubs might already have killers there, waiting expectantly for him. At three in the morning, in a driving rain, Rhyland Golden hopped a freight train headed south. Soaked to the bone and cold as ice, he collapsed in a corner of the dirty boxcar. A giant hole began to tear in Rhyland's heart. Each forlorn wail of the locomotive whistle took him further and further away from his dearly loved family that he knew he would never see again.

Storge

Storge is the natural love of family. Storge is most evident in the love of parents for their children and grandparents for their grandchildren. Children's love for their mother is strongest in early life. However, children's love for their father is often only realized in full measure after their father has died.

Regan ||

Rose Golden woke up alone the morning after Rhyland's abrupt departure, in an emotional free fall. Despite being in a state of shock, she began to take simple steps to reestablish her life without her husband and best friend. She called her neighborhood friend Briana Emeralde and they went to lunch at the Blue Sparrow diner. Rose shared that her husband had gone on a business trip to Maimi. Briana's husband had recently lost his business. They commiserated upon finding each other in hard life circumstances. Just having someone to talk to went a long way for Rose. Rose and Briana became a team after that meeting, each helping the other get through some very difficult days.

After several days, Rose started seeing an unfamiliar black car in her rearview mirror. The children reported seeing a black car down the block with a man in it looking at their house with binoculars, and they were scared. About a week after Rhyland's departure, Rose heard a knock at the front door. Upon opening the door, she was confronted by two police detectives. The detective proceeded to stridently inquire as to the where-abouts of her husband. She told the detectives that her husband had gone on a business trip to Miami and that she had not heard from him since his departure.

The dark mood that Rose initially experienced continued to darken. She went to confession, revealing to the priest that her husband had left her and that the loss had devastated her. The priest instructed her to receive communion every Sunday for the rest of the year. In taking communion during the proceeding months, Rose began to experience relief from her dark mood.

Rose Golden, left with six children, began to look for things to sell. The paid-for Lincoln went first. The acre home site on the hilltop took some time but eventually was sold to a wealthy couple from France. She pinched pennies as best she could, but eventually, the money ran out.

Rose looked across the room at her old, reliable Singer Sewing Machine and realized what she had to do. She went door to door and found sewing jobs. The jobs were small at first, but soon, she became a respected seamstress, creating flawless fashions for the few remaining wealthy women in town. Rose Golden never remarried.

Marin Golden dropped out of college and went to New York City to find a job. Marin eventually fell out of contact with the family. Fiona Golden met and married a man from Baltimore. Due to the fact that he was a Protestant, the other girls disowned her. The remaining three Golden girls shunned men and never married.

Regan Golden grew up a lonely boy, always looking back to the times when he played catch with his Dad. Regan tried but never really had any interest in schoolwork, preferring to play army in the woods with his best buddy, Tom Emeralde.

Father in the Home

The absence of a father in the home has adverse physical and behavioral consequences for a growing child. The loss of a father negatively affects the length of telomeres, the protective nucleoprotein end caps of chromosomes. At *ten years of age, children who had lost their fathers had significantly shorter telomeres than children with their fathers in the home. These effects were mor pronounced for boys than girls. (10)*

Genetics III

In 1869, Friedrich Miescher, a Swiss chemist, discovered an odd substance while researching the protein components inside the nuclei of white blood cells. In performing proteolysis on these proteins, Miescher observed that one compound was highly resistant to proteolysis. This compound had a higher phosphorous content than the rest. Miescher's high phosphorous compound, which he called 'nuclein,' was later renamed nucleic acid. He came t the realization that he had encountered a unique chemical entity. Miescher postulated that a whole family of these high phosphorous containing substances would eventually be discovered.

Phoebus Levene, a Russian-born American biochemist, studied the structure and function of nucleic acid. Levene identified two unique compounds, ribose, and deoxyribose. Ribose was later determined to be the carbohydrate component of ribonucleic acid (RNA). Deoxyribose was later found to be the carbohydrate component of deoxyribonucleic acid (DNA). I his subsequent research, Levene delineated the chemical formulas of both RNA and DNA.

Erwin Chargaff, an Austrian biochemist, expanded upon Miescher and Levene's foundational efforts. Chargaff noted that DNA composition varie with species. Chargaff determined that the content of Adenine and Thymin

DNA were equal. Chargaff also determined that the content of Guanine
d Cytosine were equal in DNA.

The organic chemist Alexander Todd determined that the backbone of
e DNA molecule contained repeating groups of phosphate and
oxyribose. The discovery of DNA and its structure was the result of many
cades of multifaceted exploration by many highly gifted researchers.

It took a woman, however, to ferret out the major scientific clues to the
lical structure of DNA. Rosalind Franklin, at Kings College in London,
ovided some of the most critical discoveries in DNA research. Franklin
lized X-Ray diffraction imaging to derive (crystallographic) structural
pictions of DNA. Franklin's work demonstrated that two (phosphate-
oxyribose) backbones were located on the outside of the molecule. Franklin
o delineated that DNA had all the structural characteristics of a helix.

Linus Pauling proposed a three stranded helical DNA model that was
ickly determined to be erroneous. James Watson and Francis Crick at
ambridge University conducted no experiments of their own on DNA.
ther, they copied Linus Pauling's cardboard modeling technique to compare
ferent shapes. Franklin's research convinced Watson and Crick that the
uctural form of DNA was that of a helix. After endlessly comparing
ferent cardboard cutout structural options, they developed a double helix
uctural model for DNA. Crick figured out that the two DNA backbones
re antiparallel. Then, by considering Chargaff's base pair findings, Crick
monstrated that the base pairs interlocked in the middle of the double helix to
ep the distance between the chains constant.

In 1953, Watson and Crick published a paper describing the double he

structure of DNA. The publication of this paper was a seminal event in the

history of biological science and gave rise to a wholly elevated understanding

biological life. The aggregate of these findings was the consequence of inten

research by many scientists over the better part of a century. The result has

been an explosion of new research and development that continues to this da

to reorder and improve the life of the average person.

Rosalind Franklin remained friends with both Watson and Crick until h

untimely death from ovarian cancer in 1958. The world lost a Lady of true

nobility. In 1962, the Nobel Prize for Medicine was awarded to James Wats

and Francis Crick for their double helix model of DNA. Watson and Crick,

as evidence of their lack of basic civility, gave scant acknowledgment to

Franklin's groundbreaking discoveries as the essential foundation for their

modeling. (11), (12), (13), (14), (15), (16), (17), (18).

The Ovaries

The female reproductive anatomy has a great deal more complexity tha

that of the male. In addition to producing eggs, her body must prepare to

nurture the fertilized egg (developing child) for nine months. This anatomy

consists of four major components; the ovaries, the fallopian tubes, the uterus

and the vagina.

The paired ovaries, located on either side of the uterus, are the primar

reproductive organs of the female, serving as the female gonads. Like the ma

gonads, the ovaries serve a dual purpose. The ovaries not only produce egg but they also produce the female sex hormones estrogen and progesterone. Unlike men, women are born with all their eggs (primary follicles) contained within the ovaries.

The ovarian cycle is composed of three phases: the follicular phase, the ovulatory phase, and the luteal phase. The follicular phase involves the maturation of the primordial follicle into a vesicular follicle. In the ovulatory phase, the ovarian wall ruptures, and the mature egg is expelled into the peritoneal cavity. In the luteal phase, the ovary forms the corpus luteum out of the remnants of the vesicular follicle. The corpus luteum then begins to secrete progesterone and some estrogen. If impregnation occurs the hormonal function of the corpus luteum continues until the placenta is fully formed and its hormonal output begins. If impregnation does not occur, the corpus luteum begins to degenerate in about ten days, and its hormonal output eventually ceases.

The ovary is flanked by two fallopian tubes, which form the initial structures of the female duct system. They receive the ovulated (expelled) egg and provide a site where fertilization can occur. The ovarian aspect of the fallopian tubes (the infundibulum of the greater ampulla) forms what resembles a hand with multiple fingers (fimbriae). These fimbriae drape over the ovary but have little or no contact with the ovary itself. The fimbriae become very active during ovulation and undulate to sweep the ovary. The beating cilia on the fimbriae create currents in the peritoneal fluid that carry the egg into the tube. Once inside the fallopian tube, the egg is carried toward the uterus by a combination of peristalsis and the rhythmic beating of the cilia. (19).

Ovarian Cancer

Ovarian cancers were previously believed to begin only in the ovaries. However, it has been recently discovered that some ovarian cancers may actually start in the cells at the ovarian end of the fallopian tubes. The ovaries and the fallopian tubes are, for the most part, made up of three kinds of cells. Each type of cell can develop into a different type of tumor. Epithelial tumors start from the cells that cover the outer surface of the ovaries and the fallopian tubes. Most ovarian tumors are epithelial cell tumors. Germ cell tumors start from the cells that produce the eggs (ova). Stromal tumors start from structural tissue cells that hold the ovary together. These tumors produce the female hormones estrogen and progesterone.

Some of these tumors are benign (non-cancerous) and never spread beyond the ovary. Malignant (cancerous) or borderline (low malignant potential) ovarian tumors can spread (metastasize) to other parts of the body and can be fatal. Cancerous epithelial tumors are called carcinomas. About 85% of malignant ovarian cancers are epithelial ovarian carcinomas. (20).

Eiryanna III

In her High School years, despite the Depression hitting her hometown hard, Eiryanna Emeralde had visions of becoming a social worker. Many of the girls in her class had gotten pregnant and had eloped with their boyfriends. Many boys in her class had to drop out of school to help their dad put food on he table. Her younger brother Tom's best buddy Regan had lost his dad. Regan's family maintained that he had died while on a business trip to Florida. The rumor around town was that he had simply run off and abandoned his family.

After graduating High School, Eiryanna applied to the University of Connecticut at Mansfield. Toward the middle of July, the postman delivered a letter from the University of Connecticut. Eiryanna was overcome with a mixture of fear and expectation. She asked her mother, Briana, and her sister, Mary, to sit down with her at the kitchen table. Not knowing what to expect she pulled the letter from the envelope and handed it to her mother to read while she crossed her fingers and closed her eyes. Her mother unfolded the letter, and suddenly, a big smile came across her face as she exclaimed, "It says here you have been accepted for the Fall semester at the University of Connecticut at Mansfield." Eiryanna and Mary immediately jumped up, gave a loud cheer, and began dancing around the table. "Well, well, fantastic, we will have to bake a cake and celebrate with all the family tonight," proclaimed Briana.

During her first semester at college, Eiryanna joined a sorority and met her lifelong, 'partner in crime,' Chris. Chris was the 'Spitting Image' of a popular movie star of the day. Together, they became unstoppable and were at every party on campus that Fall. Halfway through her glorious first semester, Eiryanna was called to the Dean's office. The Dean wasted no time in telling her that if she didn't knuckle down and start making better grades, she would not be asked to return for the Spring semester.

It was "Katy bar the Door," and Eiryanna disappeared into the Library. Eiryanna finished the semester with a GPA just barely high enough to get her to the Spring semester. She and Chris threw a party! At that party, she met Ed Clark, the Governor's son, who was to be her paramour throughout he college years.

In the spring of 1938, during her last semester at college, Eiryanna and Ed came to a fork in the road. Ed wanted to get married and go to work for hi dad, the Governor. Eiryanna wanted to accept a recent job offer as a Social Worker in San Diego, California. As a Social Worker, she could live out he dream of becoming an independent, self-reliant female. When Chris snagged a job on Coronado Island in San Diego, the deal was done, and the dynamic du were off on a new adventure.

In the Fall of 1938, San Deigo was a New England girl's fantasy come true. Warm in the day but never hot, cool in the evening but never cold. Endless beautiful beaches with lots of palm trees and all the bright sunshine in the world. The houses and businesses were all well-kept, with gardens of flowers encircling everything. The people were well-dressed and very friendly. There were restaurants of every variety lining the beach. Handsome Marines and Sailors in their immaculately tailored dress uniforms were everywhere. Eiryanna and Chris soon became the talk of the town, always present at the nightclubs of choice where only Officers were allowed.

On December 7, 1941, the Empire of Japan attacked Pearl Harbor, and the United States entered World War II. Everything in San Deigo began to change very rapidly. The streets became packed with heavy trucks delivering war supplies headed to the Pacific Front. With rifles on their shoulders, companies of combat-dressed soldiers could be seen marching up and down the streets, on the beaches, and in the open fields. The restaurants and nightclubs became virtually deserted as the call to duty required very long ys and no weekends. The good times came to an abrupt halt. Ships began arrive carrying flag-draped caskets destined for the heartland.

Empathy 1

The differences between empathy, sympathy, and compassion are subtle t very important. Empathy is an emotive assumption of what the observer lieves the observed is feeling, ascertained mainly by reading their facial pressions. In empathy, the person does not actually feel the other person's otional pain. The empathetic individual subjectively recalls the feeling of eir own pain experience in a similar circumstance. They then relate their pain what they assume the actual subject is experiencing.

Sympathy is a cognitive (logical) assumption of what the other person is st likely experiencing. When you are sympathetic, you are not actually periencing the sensory pain or emotional suffering of another. In sympathy, u are able to objectively understand the situation the person is in and realize pain they are most probably experiencing.

Compassion is the willingness to relieve the suffering of another. In mpassion, you enlist both sympathy and empathy to gain the motivation to eliorate or fully alleviate the subject's pain and suffering. A genuinely mpassionate individual steps out of the formal/subjective realm into the terial/objective realm of task initiation and successful task completion. They this to solve the underlying cause of the other person's pain and suffering.), (22), (23), (24).

Eiryanna IV

Eiryanna's workload became intense. As the men went to war, their wiv[...]
had to go to work, and their young children had to be put into day care.
Daycare centers sprang up everywhere, and they were all required to be
licensed and inspected. Diapers, baby food, and cribs were all in short suppl[...]
Women needed to be trained to work in the daycare centers, and
transportation had to be arranged for the mothers. The discipline of adultho[...]
suddenly became the hard reality of Eiryanna's life. As a Yankee of hardy
Irish stock, she quickly shouldered the burden without complaint.

Chris, always the femme fatale, was dating a handsome mid-twenties
flying instructor who was a second lieutenant, and most importantly, he was n[...]
married. However, the fun of dating during the late thirties became a nightma[...]
for Eiryanna in the early forties. The only men with college degrees were
officers, and they were mostly all married. The new recruits that came throug[...]
San Deigo were teenagers who stayed for about a month and then went off [...]
war. Eiryanna was now in her late twenties and considered an old maid and a
spinstress. She got word from her sister Mary that Ed Clark had been
elected to the Legislature and had married. She often ruminated over her
decision to break-up with Ed. Perhaps she had made a colossal mistake? Th[...]
lonely, independent life was not all that it had been cracked up to be. Whatev[...]
the case, her only choice now was to make the best of it.

Women's Depression I

There are eight distinct types of depression: major depressive disorder (MDD), persistent depressive disorder (PDD), bipolar disorder (BP), seasonal affective disorder (SAD), psychotic depression (PD), Peripartum or postpartum depression (PPD), Premenstrual dysphoric disorder (PMDD), and Situational depression (SD)

Common symptoms of depression include loss of interest or pleasure in life's activities, weight gain (due to binge eating) or weight loss (due to loss of appetite), sleep disorders, restlessness, agitation, anger, sluggish physical and mental capabilities, feelings of guilt, feelings of worthlessness and hopelessness, inability to concentrate and make decisions, suicidal thoughts, and suicidal planning.

Women's and men's mental depression are vastly different in a variety of ways. Women's depression tends to be more episodic and volatile, going up and down like a roller coaster. Women's depression tends to have a shorter time frame than men's. Women are at least two times more likely than men to be diagnosed with MDD, which is one of the leading causes of mental disease burden among women. This greater numerical frequency of presentation has many social, anatomical, and physiological roots, which are only beginning to be understood in the past few decades. Women's depression begins, on average, sometime after the tenth year as the female hormone cycle begins. (25), (26), (27), (28).

Firyanna V

Eiryanna's brother Tom had a childhood buddy named Regan. Tom gave Eiryanna a call to give her a heads up that Regan was headed out to San Diego to begin his Marine Corps Boot Camp. As a favor to Tom, Eiryanna took Regan out for a tour of town and Chinese Food. Regan was three years younger than her and very unsophisticated. Regan did not have a college degree and he was a grease monkey. At least in Regan, it was refreshing to talk to a man without an irritating, slow southern drawl.

Regan's Marine Corps training ended abruptly and he was sent immediately to the Pacific Front. As the war dragged on, she thought long and hard about moving back to New England to get her doctorate so that she could teach college. Teaching college was gentrified, and college professors were always the gentlemen.

Finally, on September 2, 1945, the Empire of Japan surrendered, and the entire nation celebrated that they had finally, at a great cost, defeated evil itself. Eiryanna made plans to return to New Haven. California had lost its charm, and she longed to see her mother and father. Her father, Gareth, who had contracted malaria during the Spanish-American War, was now in poor health.

On September 28, 1945, Eiryanna's thirtieth birthday, she got a call from Regan, who had just returned to San Diego from the Pacific Front. Eiryanna, during the subsequent date, failed to inform Regan that she had just that day turned thirty. They found a quiet French café and had a delightful meal. After the waiter had been paid, Regan pulled out a small box and gave it to her. To Eiryanna's total surprise, the box contained an engagement ring. Before she could politely decline, Regan, anticipating her refusal, said, "Just think about it. I am headed back to New Haven, so there's lots of time."

Upon his return to New Haven, Regan had trouble finding work. There were hoards of men who had just gotten home from the war, and they all were seeking employment. Through a friend, he got a job driving a dump truck hauling gravel for a new road to Yonkers. The hours were long, and the pay was marginal, but he knew he was lucky to have a job. Squeezing back into the house with his mother and sisters was not working out, so he took up residence in a tool shed behind a friend's house and showered at the YMCA.

After Eiryanna had returned to New Haven, she began to look for jobs as a social worker but soon realized that there were very few openings. Soon, she took up bucket and brush, and went to work with her mother cleaning floors. During that year, Eiryanna's father died from the complications of malaria. After seeing him suffer, his death was a strange, bittersweet mixture of sadness and beautiful memories.

Eiryanna put in an application with the local Public School System and started getting a few jobs here, and there, substitute teaching for women who were with child. Eiryanna loved every minute of teaching and began to consider returning to school for her teaching certification. Eiryanna was a strict disciplinarian and made sure that every student did their homework every day. The boys hated her, and the girls loved her. The parents were happy to have a teacher who made sure their children learned their lessons.

Eiryanna and Regan began to see a lot of each other and, somewhere in the process, fell in love. About a year after returning to New Haven, they were married in a small ceremony at St Patrick's Cathedral. They soon discovered that they both had a dream of starting a restaurant. Forming a brain trust, they began to make elaborate plans to create the best restaurant in New Haven. Eiryanna's mother, Briana, had been willed a building by her mother called the

Century House. With her mother's nod of approval, Eiryanna and Regan, with high energy and great expectations, began to renovate the building to create The Century House Restaurant.

Eros

Eros is sensual Human Romantic Love that encompasses a desire for close companionship, passion, and lust.

Human Romantic Love I

Being married has a tendency to improve a person's overall health. This effect is partially due to the reality that having a long-term bond alters hormone in such a way as to mitigate stress. Marriage and the social support it provides can buffer against anxiety. Although marriage itself can be very stressful, successfully coping with marital situations makes it easier for people to handle other stressful events in their lives. Marriage has a dampening effect on the cortisol responses to psychological stress.

People who experience a higher feeling of being loved (felt love) in everyday life also have significantly higher levels of psychological well-being, which includes feelings of purpose and optimism. People with higher felt love tend to have higher extraversion (outgoing) personality scores. People with lower felt love scores were more likely to show signs of neuroticism (self-focus). (29), (30), (31), (32), (33), (34), (35).

Eiryanna VI

With grand celebration and fanfare, 'The Century House Restaurant' opened in the summer of 1946. For the first two years, it seemed like all of New Haven was at their door every evening. Everything on the menu was top drawer, and the desserts were from heaven. The local newspaper had article after article singing their praises. Eiryanna and Regan were working twelve-hour days. Six months after opening the restaurant, Eiryanna had a miscarriage. Bob insisted that Eiryanna remain home for a month, but after that time, she returned to the restaurant like gangbusters.

Chimera

Until recently, it was believed that a person has but one unique type of DNA in their body. Recent discoveries of people with two types of DNA in their bodies (chimera) have led to a plethora of new research into this phenomenon. The most extreme type of chimerism is known as the vanishing twin syndrome, in which one twin dies early in utero, and the surviving twin acquires some of the deceased twin's DNA. This phenomenon is called tetra-gametic chimerism. Additionally, regularly born fraternal twins can sometimes exchange DNA in the uterus since they have a shared blood supply.

Micro-chimerism involves mothers acquiring fetal blood cells during their pregnancy and retaining them in various organs, including their brain and heart, for many years after pregnancy. Heart failure in women shortly after birth is a common phenomenon. These cases have the best recovery rate for any type of heart failure. Researchers have discovered fetal cells circulating in the mother's heart that are thought to help repair the damage and restore the mother's heart to full health. Mothers who miscarry (and sadly never get to know that child) can many times carry the DNA of the miscarried child in their brains and their hearts for their entire life. (36), (37), (38).

Eiryanna VII

Halfway through the summer of 1948, a hard recession hit the country, and people everywhere were losing their jobs. The entire populace was gripped with fear that the Depression had returned. Within a month, the line of customers at the restaurant door disappeared. Early that Fall, Eiryanna, and Regan were forced to give up their dream, and the Century House Restaurant was closed. Regan went back to driving a gravel truck, and Eiryanna returned to substitute teaching.

After the restaurant closed, Eiryanna's fate continued to worsen. Regan's work petered out, and he soon realized that he was not going to find work in New Haven. Regan spent day after day sitting in the local library on Elm Street, endlessly combing through want ads in newspapers from all over the country. Regan eventually found hope that jobs could be found in Houston, Texas. Throwing many anxious thoughts over his shoulder, Regan drove a worn-out old dump truck to Texas and found work in Houston.

Eiryanna, now with a one-year-old daughter, hung on in New Haven as long as she could. Eiryanna knew that she had to let go of New Haven, but in her heart, she absolutely did not want to leave. Eiryanna began to question past decision-making process over and over again. Eiranna, being a college grad, realized that she had in great error, married the grease monkey.

Regan was a good man, but that good man Regan would never be a college professor. On the phone, Regan kept insisting that Eiryanna move to the wholly uncivilized frontier province of Texas. Months of refusal finally ended, and Eiryanna reluctantly followed Regan to the wild, vacant wasteland of Texas. During her early years in Texas, she had two more children, both boys.

Eiryanna found herself stranded twenty miles from Houston in an old farmhouse out on the endless flat Texas countryside. Above the kitchen sink, which incessantly dripped, was a sash window with glass panes that one could never get quite clean enough. Eiryanna was forced to realize that this old country house, which had seemed so quaint at first, was in hard reality, just a shack. She couldn't even afford a party line phone!

The view out the farmhouse window was of a two-lane tar and gravel blacktop road that stretched forever south towards Houston. Along the side of the road grew three-foot-tall Johnson grass, which was not really grass at all, just an ugly weed. Every once in a great while, one could see a twisted, drought-stricken post-oak tree. These gnarled horrors hardly compared to the mighty oak trees that gave New Haven such dignity. Everything about this awful place was primordial, unruly, and seemed cursed by the gods.

The farmhouse kitchen table was from an older dining room set Regan had purchased at a yard sale. At first, she was happy to have found it, but the more she studied it, the shabbier she realized it truly was. She remembered the elegant quarter-sawn oak dining room table that graced her father's majestic house. The thin veneer top on this table was worn at all the place settings, and the cheap chrome border had begun to pit and rust around the edges.

Each of the seven metal chairs was in a varying state of disrepair. She could hardly deny thinking of why seven chairs. Was that predictive? She hoped not! Three children were way more than enough, and now she was expecting a fourth! If she had been given a choice, she would have stopped at two. Eiryanna watched her three children, Doirann, five, Simon, three, and Ike one, from the kitchen window as they played out in the yard.

Eiryanna, feeling abandoned in this dilapidated shack, endlessly worried about the quandary she found herself in. She was nine months pregnant and expecting any day. Her thoughtless husband, Regan, had taken their only vehicle, a worn-out old Buick, to his job driving a dump truck hauling gravel for some big new highway. He could have arranged to get a ride with one of his drinking buddies so she could have had the Buick. Or, at the very least, gotten her a party line phone! But NO!

Women's Depression II

A common feature in female depression is rumination. Rumination can be described as a painful mental loop of overthinking stressful situations leading to harmful self-denigration. Research has found that this rumination takes place in a circular connection between the Posterior Cingulate Cortex (thinking area), the Right Inferior Temporal Gyrus (emotion area), and the Right Inferior Frontal Gyrus (emotion area). These zones are involved in self-referential thinking (self-focus) and negative emotional stimuli processing (selflenigration). One very successful strategy to break the endless loop of umination is to focus one's thoughts on another person with a greater need for ittention than oneself. This new focus can be on the innocence of a newborn hild or the needs of an aging relative. (25, (26), (27), (28).

Eiryanna VIII

Eiryanna's labor pains began, and she was scared. As her labor pains ncreased in severity and frequency, she realized she would have to try to make to the hospital on her own. With her youngest in arm and the other two hildren in tow, Eiryanna set off walking down the worn-out blacktop farm road outh toward Houston. After walking a long time without seeing a single car, he became distraught. Suddenly, she broke her water. Eiryanna sat down, rossed-legged on the asphalt, and began to weep silently. Her children athered around her and gave her hugs as their tears flowed onto her worn and aded house dress.

After what seemed like an eternity had passed, she began to hear the int sound of a car motor. She looked to the north to see a car in the distance eaded her way. Eventually, an ornate, long black Cadillac came to a stop eside her. An older gentleman dressed in a black tuxedo got out and made a rief inquiry. He then helped her and her children into the vehicle. Eiryanna nd her children were taken to the hospital in Houston in a hearse driven by the cal undertaker.

The Womb

The uterus is a thick-walled hollow organ that functions to receive, retain, and nourish the fertilized egg. The innermost wall of the uterus, the endometrium, has a mucosal lining that allows for the implantation of the fertilized egg. The top layer of the endometrium, the stratum functionalis, undergoes cyclic changes in response to blood levels of ovarian hormones. If a fertilized egg does not imbed after ovulation, this stratum is shed during menstruation.

The ovarian hormonal cycle has an average twenty-eight-day length. This cycle has three consecutive phases: the follicular, the ovulatory, and the luteal. At the beginning of the follicular phase of this cycle, levels of gonadotropin-releasing hormone (GnRH) from the hypothalamus begin to rise. This GnRH increase stimulates increased production and release of follicle-stimulating hormone (FSH) and luteinizing hormone (LH) by the anterior pituitary. FSH and LH stimulate follicular (egg-containing structure) growth and maturation within the ovaries. As the follicle enlarges, androgen secretion begins in the thecal cells of the follicle, which is then converted into estrogen by the granulosa cells.

The initial small rise in estrogen blood levels inhibits the hypothalamic-pituitary axis (negative feedback); however, as the estrogen levels continue to increase, they have the opposite effect (positive feedback) of stimulating that axis (the ovulatory phase). This causes a sudden flood of LH and FSH by the anterior pituitary at midcycle. This, in turn, facilitates ovulation at around day fourteen in midcycle.

During ovulation, the egg is expelled from both the sac-like follicle and e wall of the ovary in the same process. Then, the empty follicle in the ovary rms into the corpus luteum, producing mostly progesterone and some trogen (the luteal phase). The rise in progesterone has an inhibiting effect egative feedback), causing the anterior pituitary to decrease FSH and LH oduction. As the LH levels decrease, the corpus luteum degenerates.

If no uterine implantation occurs, the progesterone levels will bsequently decrease sharply. This decrease in progesterone levels causes e uterine stratum functionalis to degenerate. The stratum functionalis then ughs off and exits through the vagina as menstrual flow during the female riod (at the end of the ovarian cycle). The marked decline in ovarian rmones at the end of the cycle stops their blockade of FSH and FS cretion, causing the cycle to begin anew.

In the event of a fertilized egg attaching to the stratum functionalis erus) during the luteal phase, the corpus luteum (ovary) is maintained until the erine placenta takes over hormone production. The average time period ring which the uterine stratum functionalis is receptive to implantation is seven ys after ovulation.

The menstrual cycle has a twenty-eight-day average. This cycle involves eries of changes that the endometrium (uterus) undergoes in response to the rmonal changes during the ovarian cycle. The three phases of the uterine cle are the menstrual, the proliferative, and the secretory. The menstrual rresponds to the end of the luteal phase when the decrease in progesterone uses the stratum functionalis (uterus) to slough off. The proliferative phase rresponds to the rebuilding of the stratum functionalis before ovulation. The cretory phase begins immediately after ovulation when the increased blood supply caused by the elevated progesterone and estrogen provides the nutrients that prepare the endometrium to receive the embryo.

Before fertilization can occur, the sperm must first reach the ovulated egg. The sperm is viable for about twenty-four hours as it travels from the vagina through the uterus into the fallopian tubes. Of the millions of sperm released, only one permeates the egg. The corona radiata and the egg's zona pellucida must be breached during this process. After this breaching, the sperm makes contact with the egg membrane, where its nucleus is pulled into the egg's cytoplasm. The egg sodium channels open at that point, causing the egg membrane to depolarize. This depolarization causes the egg membrane to gain water and swell. This swelling causes all other sperm to detach from the egg membrane, ensuring only one sperm remains in the egg.

The sperm which has undergone meiosis during its formation in the male body has half of the male genetic content. When the sperm enters the egg, it remains in the peripheral cytoplasm for a short period of time. The female nucleus then undergoes meiosis II to form the ovum nucleus, which contains half of the female's genetic content. The ovum nuclei and the sperm nuclei swell, becoming the female and male pronuclei. Both pronuclei are drawn towards each other as a mitotic spindle develops between them. Both pronuclei then rupture, releasing their chromosomes into the immediate vicinity of the spindle.

The actual moment of fertilization occurs as the maternal and paternal chromosomes combine, forming the diploid zygote. As soon as the diploid zygote is formed, the combined chromosomes join. After this joining, the cell has either XX or XY sex chromosomes, and that individual person's biological sex is determined for life. The joined chromosomes then replicate by the mitotic process and the first cell division occurs.

The placenta is a temporary organ that originates from both embryonic and maternal tissues. Its primary function is to connect the fetal blood supply with the maternal blood supply's nutritive, respiratory, excretory, and endocrine elements. This allows the developing child's body to grow exponentially in the womb. The child's development is rapid and amazing in its complexity. On average, by day 28, the child has a heartbeat. There are children who were only 21 weeks in the womb who have survived birth and lived.

There are three stages of labor; dilation, expulsion, and placental. The dilatation stage begins with the first uterine contraction and continues until the baby's head fully dilates the cervix (about 10 cm in diameter). As the baby's head is pushed against the cervix, the cervix softens and dilates. The dilation phase can last twelve or more hours. Eventually, the amnion ruptures, and the amnionic fluid is released in an event known as "the breaking of the water." Expulsion is the actual birth of the child and can be sudden or take many hours. (19)

Eiryanna IX

Several months after the birth of her fourth child, at Eiryanna's staunch insistence, she and Regan moved to a brand-new house in a suburb west of Houston. This track housing development had next-door neighbors, a cement sidewalk, a front yard, and an ample backyard. Eiryanna had adamantly concluded that she was never, under any circumstance, going to live in the outback ever again. She was beyond elation to be back in something that resembled civilization. In time, Eiryanna had a fifth child, another boy.

Kid Stories 1

The date was Saturday, September 8, 1956, and after a long, hot summer, the weather had finally begun to cool. Like all young men in the 1950's, I was a car nut. Males, in the very modern era, were driven to spend vast amounts of time becoming experts on the evolution of car design. It had been mutually agreed upon by my brothers and I that the 1955 Chevrolet was the coolest car ever made. Further, we concluded that the 1956 Chevy grille was, at best, a big let-down. Although preliminary drawings of the 1957 Chevrolet had been released, the nation was going to have to wait until December to get a real first-hand look. People everywhere were firmly convinced that the future of the free world was definitely at stake in the 1957 Chevrolet design.

I was getting older and would be four in the coming April. The Fall had arrived; the sky was clear blue, butterflies were dancing everywhere, the birds were out on the wire, and love was in the air. In the yard of the house across the street, twin girls were playing in their sandbox. As usual, they invited me to play with them. They were playing kitchen and fixed me a wonderful meal of leaves, pebbles, and twigs. It was, of course, a formal affair with all the required silverware and stuff. After the hearty meal, I graciously thanked my hosts and wiped my mouth with a new leaf.

The after-twig brunch conversation turned to the wonders of romance. "Love Me Tender," by Elvis, was all over the radio that Summer. The twins and I discussed what it meant to love someone tender. The first twin, Susie, was a bit of a snob and thought that love was utterly silly. I had a head-over-heels crush on the other twin, Katie. Katie expounded at length and concluded that if two people were in love, it was only proper that they should get married. I was thunderstruck, and my heart melted right there on the spot. About that time, I heard Mother calling for lunch from across the street, and I was hungry for real food.

Mother announced at lunch that Elvis Presley was going to be on the Ed Sulivan show tomorrow night. A loud discussion, verging on an all-out argument, ensued. My brother Simon, being seven and very mature, thought that Elvis was a one-time wonder and that Frank Sinatra was the real talent. He thought that Pat Boone was the real deal. I wasn't quite so sure but was willing to give Elvis a shot. We were all very excited but soon realized that it was a moot point because we did not own a TV set.

After lunch, we went out into the backyard, built a quick fort, and started to play war. The no TV conundrum was on everybody's mind, and our lack of enthusiasm for war soon became apparent. We sat down on a board and began to seek a solution. Harold, the kid in the house across the street, next to the twins, had a TV; in fact, it was a color TV. However, his parents didn't like us because we were Catholics. Therefore, asking if we could watch Ed Sulivan at their house was out of the question. "I know it," said Ike. "There's a window next to their garage that looks into their living room, which is pointed right straight at their TV."

Logistics were then discussed. The window was very high and we would need a box to stand on. Shortly after that realization, we three were on our wa six blocks north to the nearest grocery store, the B&B. When we got to the back of the B&B, we found several wood-slat orange crates in the garbage cans. We selected two and quickly returned to the house. After dismantling the most wobbly crate, we began to straighten out the nails on a flat rock with our claw hammer. We used the nails and the slats to reinforce the remaining crate so that it would be fit for standing on.

Sunday morning came with all the same tedious requirements. We were forced to wear those ugly dress-up clothes. Black cotton slacks that required ironing. A white cotton long-sleeve shirt that required ironing. The shirt had a tight-necked collar, and a black clip-on bow tie was also mandated. This get-u made a self-respecting tough guy look like a sissy. The worst was having to sit at attention and listen to that boring old Italian priest drone on and on half the morning.

After eons of time had elapsed, Sunday afternoon arrived, and the commando planning ensued. The Ed Sulivan Show came on at seven in the evening, a little before sunset. Elvis would probably come on before seven-thirty. We had to have a spy to look from a distance to determine the exact tim of his appearance. Then, with Harold's family firmly glued to the TV set, we would rush over with our box and set up our observation post. It was imperativ that silence be maintained and that we take turns, by age, standing on the box.

As dusk began to fall, Simon set up his lookout post. At his signal, Ike and I rushed over with the watch tower. Simon first, then Ike, finally, at last, I stood on the perch and peered into Harold's living room. I had a clear view of that modern electronic wonder, Harold's Color Television Set. Elvis was

esmerizing as his deep, sultry voice filled the earth with "Love me tender, Love
 true,"

Suddenly, my time was up. Ike and Simon began trying to pull me off the
 x. I clung to the window sill and would not budge until life had been completed
 d The Mighty Elvis finished the very last note of "Love Me Tender.".
inally, they began to slug me, and I let go of the sill, falling backwards along
th the box. The fall made a bunch of noise, and instantly, a light went on in
 arold's living room. We raced back across the street to our house with the
 x and hid behind a big cedar tree. Over at Harold's house, the front porch
 ht went on, and his father came out to investigate. Finding nothing, he soon
 nt back inside, and both lights went out. We had pulled it off! The Elvis
 aper had been an unrivaled success!

The next day was clear and bright. All the women were out on the
 ewalk talking about Elvis. Some feigned disgust at his vulgar body
 ovements but most lustfully sang his praises. I returned to my Katie, barely
 lding back the floodgates of my heart as we played Jaxs. Finally, when I
 uld no longer constrain the tidal wave within my heart, I confessed to Katie
 at I loved her tender and I loved her true. Immediately, I went down on one
 ee and asked her to marry me. She graciously accepted, and we held hands
 rever.

Susie, being the pill she always had to be, began to deride the entire
 air. Katie, being true, began to plan the wedding and make a list. She had to
 ve a gown, there had to be a ring, and so on went the list. The gown was a
 owcase off the line, the ring was a washer, and Susie reluctantly agreed to be
 preacher. In those days, all girls knew the vows. When all was set, we faced
 ch other and repeated after Susie; to have and to hold, for better or worse,

for richer or poorer, to love and to cherish all the days of our lives until death c
us part. The wedding hug lasted an eternity, then it was over. Immediately, I
realized that now I needed to find a job. About a month later, without notice,
Katie and her parents moved out of town.................................... And my
wonderous Katie was gone forever!

Human Romantic Love II

Human Romantic Love (HRL) is one of the most sought-after outcom
in the life of the average individual. A recently researched hormone,
Kisspeptin, has been found to initiate the release of reproductive hormones i
the body. Kisspeptin works by enhancing activity in brain structures associat
with romance. The brain area that is most involved when a person has "just
fallen madly in love" is the <u>Right Ventral Tegmental Area</u>. This brain area is
rich in another hormone, dopamine, which is an essential part of the brain's
motivation and reward system. Elevated levels of dopamine produce energy,
focus attention on novel stimuli, motivate to win a reward, and, most importantl
produce feelings of elation. All of these effects are core characteristics of
HRL.

Persons who have recently lost their love interest, on average, report th
they were still intensely "In Love" with the absent person. These individuals
tend to spend the majority of their waking hours thinking of that person and
yearning for their return.

The primary brain area involved in HRL loss was found to be the <u>Righ</u>
<u>Ventral Tegmental Area.</u> Other brain areas affected by the loss of love are

the Nucleus Accumbens and Orbitofrontal/Prefrontal Cortex. These areas are associated with craving and addiction, specifically the dopaminergic reward system. Additional areas affected by loss of love are the Insular Cortex and the Anterior Cingulate. These areas are associated with physical pain and distress. There is, however, evidence that "time heals all wounds." An area of the brain associated with attachment, the Right Ventral Putamen-Pallidum Area, displays evidence of decreasing activity as time passes after the loss of love. The takeaway is that researchers have just begun to scratch the surface of the mental processes that take place in the loss of HRL. (29), (30), (31), (32), (33), (34), (35).

Philia

Brotherly Love - Strong Friendship

Kid Stories 2

It was a warm afternoon, late in the spring of 1957, and I had just turned four in our small town in Texas. The west side of town, on the other side of Center Street, was where the white-collar people lived in beautiful brick houses. My neighborhood, east of Center Street, was the blue-collar side of town where the factories and the corrugated metal garages were. Our house was in a post-war housing tract of wood frame structures. The exterior of the houses were finished with 105 pine siding, and the paint on most houses was in various states of disrepair. Some houses had neatly mowed yards. Most of the other yards were overgrown with Johnson grass and other weeds.

My brother Ike, five, and I were out in the backyard attempting to knock down a giant yellow jacket nest built in the corner of the eve. Our chosen method of attack was precisely hurled stones we had gathered from the backyard. In the instant that Ike's rock hit the stem, the nest began to fall, yellow jackets were everywhere, and we were on a dead run for our very lives.

Knocking down a yellow jacket nest with a rock was very high on the brag list for a Texas kid. While reveling over Ike's prize nest later in the afternoon, the talk turned to profitable capitalistic ventures. As kids from the hard side of town, we were required to get our own money as soon as we could walk. We began to discuss the viability of a new business enterprise. This venture would consist of knocking down yellow jacket nests for people on the block to raise badly needed revenue. As a fair price for the service, we settled on fifty cents for big nests and a quarter for the little ones.

The next day, we went from house to house, looking for nests. Cold calls are always a problematic sales approach, but we had no other choice. About half of the people would yell at us to get the "blank" off their property. Our ace in the hole was that the little old ladies were afraid that the yellow jackets would get in their houses. We eventually found a willing customer with a big nest right on her front porch. The next day, we knocked it down and split our fifty cents. With great haste, I went down to the local Rexall Drug Store and spent my quarter on candy. Ike was determined to save his.

The following week brought burgeoning success to our new enterprise. The word spread rapidly, on the party line telephones, that the yellow jacket problem had a solution. We were up and down the block all week long with our bag of carefully selected stones. By the end of the week, we were becoming quite wealthy. However, we were beginning to exhaust the supply of nests on our block. By the second week, we knew we would have to expand our territory to sustain our momentum. We found many nests as we explored the surrounding streets and stayed busy all week. Ike and I seriously discussed franchising our newly created empire. We were determined to make a million.

That Sunday night, we counted our fortune in the secrecy of our bedroom as the parents remained uninformed about our corporate enterprise. I had three dollars and twenty-five cents, and Ike had three dollars and seventy-five cents, all in quarters. The next day, at a house two streets away, we found a huge nest. The nest was up on the flat soffit in the corner where the garage joined the house. We threw stones at the nest for a while without success. Finally, Ike took precise aim and hurled a large flat stone, hitting the nest exactly in the center. Angry yellow jackets went everywhere. We ran like the wind, but the bees flew faster. I got stung on the left forearm, so I spit on it and rubbed it in. We both laughed about it in the safety of the far sidewalk. After picking up our two quarters, we headed home victoriously.

By the time we got to the house, my left arm had started to swell. When we came into the house Mom noticed my arm in an instant. Mom began the Spanish Inquisition, and eventually, we had to lay out the whole truth. By that time, my arm had swole up like a watermelon. Eiryanna was very worried because she knew that bee stings could cause sudden death in children. Then I got really sick and had to run to the bathroom, where I heaved into the commode for what seemed like an hour.

Dad had taken the car to work, so Mom got a neighbor, Mrs Ruth, to take her and I to the doctor's office. By the time we got to the doctor, I was having trouble breathing. I heard the doctor tell Mom that I was having some sort of reaction that started with an A, and I needed to get a shot. After the doctor gave me the shot, he put a mask over my face with tubes that gave me oxygen. Sometime later, I started feeling better, and they let me go home. When Dad got home, he and Mom both read us the riot act, and that was the end of our glorious hopes of fame and fortune.

Kids Stories 3

My fifth birthday had come and gone and it was getting warm late in the Texas spring of 1958. Heavy spring rains had left tall Johnson grass in most of the yards on our block, including ours. Eiryanna, our mom, had taken on the task of mowing the yard as Dad was always at work putting food on the table. On this particular Saturday morning, Mom got out the mower for the first time that year and began to change the oil. The mower had a four-stroke Briggs & Stratton motor that sputtered and banged when it first started up. Mom showed us how to check the oil and fill the gas tank without spilling gas all over the place. Mom showed us how to pull the starter chord correctly, not too soft and not too hard. Mom showed us how to set the choke wide open to get the motor started and then how to gradually decrease the choke as the engine warmed up.

Mom showed us how to go ahead of where we were going to mow and get any rocks and other stuff out of our chosen path to prevent damage to the blade. Mom showed us how to mow in a straight line and not to push too fast the tall grass so as to keep the motor from stalling. Mom showed us how to go back and forth over the tall grass to get it mowed down good. Mom showed us

ow to plan out the yard ahead of time and divide it into rectangles so that we
ould mow in a steady, constant path.

Mom then mowed three rectangles in our front yard and three in our
ackyard. Mom gave each of us a rectangle to mow, beginning with Simon, the
dest. Mom walked the first loop with Simon, then let him finish the rectangle
 his own. Mom did the same with Ike and then me. Mom had us push the
ower to the backyard, and we repeated the process.

After the entire yard was completely mowed, we all went in and ate
ologna sandwiches and drank cokes. In the discussion that followed, Mom
ducated us in the art of how to go about estimating the price we would charge
 mow a yard. The first task was to figure out how big the yard was. She had
ach of us walk across the kitchen floor and count our steps. Then, she
owed us how to figure out how long our average step was. Simon, of course,
d the longest step. After dividing the yard into rectangles, we would walk out
e width and length of each rectangle. Simon knew how to multiply the width
nes the length because he was real smart. Simon knew how to add up each
ctangle area to give us of the size of each yard. Simon made A's in school.

The next task was to consider the average height of the grass in each
rd. That was tough because, most times, it varied across the yard. Then we
d to consider how much stuff we would have to move in order to mow the yard
oroughly, getting all the odd spaces. Mom had us set the starting price at two
llars and fifty cents per average yard. We could add quarters for all the other
rd stuff.

Mom told us that she was going to let us use the mower to start a lawn
owing company that summer. Mom told us with a stern face never to put our

fingers anywhere near the bottom of the mower while it was running. For any reason on earth! Mom told us that before we did any work on the mower, we had to detach the sparkplug wire first. Mom stated that she expected us to treat her mower as if we had to purchase it out of our own money. Mom shook all three of our hands to finalize the deal.

The next Monday, we began to go house to house on our block, ringing the doorbells of the houses with overgrown yards. Sometime after lunch, we found an old lady who wanted her yard mowed. After stepping it off and doing our estimate, we decided we should stick with the base price two fifty, just to get our first yard. Upon Simon informing the woman of our price, she stated emphatically, "TWO FIFTY, That's Highway Robbery." Simon argued with her for some time but realized his negotiation wasn't going anywhere.

Simon stated politely, "Well, ma'am, that's our lowest price, so if you change your mind, we'll be down at 1611." He turned and made it off the porch and halfway down the driveway when we heard a "wait a minute" from the lady. She then agreed to pay us two fifty "But Not A Cent More." We were all elated, and I kept asking Simon, "How did you know? How did you know." "I just had a feeling," was Simon's response.

The next morning, we brought our mower and gas can to the lady's house and began mowing her yard. It was an average-sized yard with a few tall weeds, the back and some old boards that needed moving, but nothing really hard. Simon, Ike, and I removed all the rocks, then mowed three rectangles in the front and three in the back, like mom had showed us how. I was very eager to prove myself and could hardly wait to mow my front yard rectangle. On my first row, stalled the mower, pushing it too fast, and had to endure the jeers of my brothers. After I got the mower going again, I was careful to progress at a steady pace. Mowing that first rectangle was one of the outstanding accomplishments of my already long life.

When we were finished, we rang the doorbell, and the lady appeared. She went out and surveyed the front and back and stated, "My Mother Could Have Done A Better Job." She went back inside and reappeared at the door with a jar of change. She proceeded to pay us in dimes, nickels, and pennies. She stated with finality, "I Still Say Two Fifty Is Way TOO Much," then slammed the door in our faces. The three of us strutted home like Ceasar, marching into Rome. We decided that we each should get fifty cents and put the last dollar in a jar for gas and mower repair.

That first month, we were mowing two or three yards a week, and we were on top of the world. Dad told us that a guy he worked with, Mr Brittain, wanted his yard mowed but that it was several blocks away. Dad gave us directions and told us we would have to go there tomorrow evening and negotiate the price. The next day, we went up there as the sun was beginning to set, and we introduced ourselves as Mr Golden's kids. We then proceeded to pace off the yard and do an estimate. It was a very big yard with lots of tall weeds in the backyard, so we decided it would be our first three-fifty charge. With great apprehension, we rang the bell. Simon told him the three-fifty asking price with a slight question in the inflection of his voice. With a big smile on his face, Mr Brittain said, "Great," then he invited us all in for cokes.

The next day, we got there really early because we knew it was going to get hot later on. We removed all the rocks, moved some boards in the back, and mowed six rectangles. About halfway through the very overgrown yard, three really big boys showed up. They came over into Mr Brittain's yard from the house next door with very menacing looks on their faces. They lined up against us, and the biggest one yelled: "We're the Dodge Boys, don't know if y'all have heard of us yet, but this is our yard to mow, and if you don't get your skinny butts out of here right now we're gonna haven't teach y'all not to mess with the Dodge Boys." Simon got in the biggest one's face and firmly stated, "Mr Brittain gave us this yard to mow so take that fat trailer your towing and hit the skids or y'all gonna be the ones who learn a very hard lessin."

The big one went back a step with fear in his eyes. "We're headed to the store, and y'all better be long gone by the time we get back or else," he yelled. They walked off muttering to themselves, and we went back to mowing Mr Brittain's tall grass. At one point, the Johnson grass was so thick and tall that we had to take Dad's sling blade to chop it down to where it could be mowed. Finally, we got the entire yard well-mowed. Just then, the "Dodge Boys" could be seen coming down the street.

The "Dodge boys" got to the yard as we were wrapping things up. The big one yelled, "I thought I told ya.." Before he could finish his threat, Simon got in his face, grabbed a paper bag out of his hand, and threw it over the far fence. "That's my candy," he yelled as he took a swing. Simon ducked and punched him in the gut. Simon and the big guy proceeded to slug it out. Simon, who had quicker fists and better aim, began taking him apart. The other two came after me and Ike. Ike was real good at bare knuckles and kept slamming his opponent in the kisser without even being touched. My guy was older and way bigger than me so I wrasseled him to the ground and punched him as we wrasseled. Simon threw a roundhouse, hitting the big one square in the jaw and knocking him to the ground. He got up dazed and stumbled slowly towards their house, with the other two following him, beaten and confused.

About that time, a cop car rolled up! The graying cop got out and asked us what was up. So, Simon told him, "Officer, we were minding our own business, mowing the yard Mr Brittain had told us to mow, when these guys next door came over and started trouble. The "Dodge Boys" had washed all up and changed shirts before they came out to talk with the cop. The big one ould be heard saying, "We were just being friendly when those mean boys tarted trouble by taking my candy sack and throwing it way over the fence. I want my candy back." Then he started to cry. We could hear the cop state, The next time you punks start any more trouble, I'll make sure you end up in Gainesville Reform School with that brother of yours." The cop walked back ver to us, looked over the yard, and said, "Good mowing, keep up the good ork. Better get back home. I'll take care of these jerks." We thanked the Officer, picked up our stuff, and headed back to our block, marching iumphantly as the newly crowned "Kings of the Neighborhood."

Male Aggression

It has been well documented, across all human cultures, that males are, on verage, more aggressive and less nurturing than females. Research has emonstrated that the male Y sex chromosome is the major contributor to the roduction of testosterone. The male hormone testosterone has been shown o be the major factor in the aggressive presentation of males. Men's upper ody muscle mass and, therefore, strength is between fifty and seventy-five ercent greater than that of a female. Testosterone builds a completely ifferent body type than estrogen. (39).

Kid Stories 4

The Summer of my fifth year was winding down. My brothers and I had mowed a lot of yards, and we were quite wealthy. My brothers were going to have to be in school soon, Ike for the first time. School was just a vague concept rattling around in my brain without any form or substance. Mom's lady friend, two houses down, Mrs. Ruth, invited Mom and us kids to go with her and her three kids for a picnic at Paddle Wheel Park.

Mrs. Ruth had a long station wagon with a drop-down tailgate that you could sit on while she drove. It was crazy fun. We boys devised a plan. As soon as we arrived at the Park and the car slowed down, we would hop off the tailgate, turn around in mid-air, and hit the ground on the run. It worked as planned, and what an absolute kick it was.

Paddle Wheel Park was the most beautiful Park in town, with lots of big oa trees for shade, picnic tables, and a huge lake right in the middle. We played army all morning with Paul, Mrs. Ruth's son, who was Simon's age. The Park had the neatest charcoal grills. So, we got out the charcoal briquettes, poured lots of starter fluid on them, then stood back and started throwing lit wood matches at the grill until 'poof' it went off to a loud cheer from all. Grilled hot dogs with lots of stuff on them have got to be a kid's best food.

After lunch, us boys went to the lake and began to make destroyers out o dead tree branches. A massive naval battle ensued, in which many sailors lost their lives. Tree climbing then became the focus. Oak trees are great climbing trees because their limbs are very strong, allowing a kid to get way up high. Then we went back to the lake, trying to catch minnows with our bare hands. Now that the charcoal had burned down, it became time for marshmallow roasting. Roasting a marshmallow on a coat hanger is an art that takes years to perfect. If you get it too close, it turns black and falls off the hanger. If you keep it too far away, the inside doesn't get gooey. So, we all debated the finesse of the art as we roasted the confection and stuffed our faces. The shadows became long, and with great regrets, we knew it was getting time to go ome. We helped Mrs. Ruth and Mom pack up, and we got back on the station agon tailgate and headed home.

The ride home, sitting on the tailgate dangling our legs in the cool evening eeze, was spectacular. The day had been the perfect ending to the perfect ummer. We had so much fun jumping off the tailgate the first time we decided do it again just before we got to the house. Mrs. Ruth turned down our ock, and we approached the house slowly.
he last thing I remember was jumping....

I woke up, and my head was throbbing with unbelievable pain. Reaching up, ere was something like cloth wrapped around my head. Looking around, I und I was in some weird type bed with shiny steel rails on the side. From the her room, I heard a man's voice declare, "I have to tell you, Mrs. Golden, it's a racle of God that your son is even alive; his head was cracked open like an g. By all medical standards, he should be dead; however, other than the anial fracture, which will heal, he seems to be ok." Eiryanna entered the room d approached my bed. Upon seeing that I was awake, she bent over and ftly kissed my cheek, wetting my face with her tears.

Eiryanna X

Regan was a hard worker, but as the economy went up and down in the ties, he experienced one layoff after another. With a wife, five kids, and a rtgage, he would have to find work quickly after every layoff. One evening, ile driving a cab in Houston for a dollar an hour plus tips, Regan picked up a e to the Men's Cub, a striptease joint. When he had dropped off his ssenger, the owner of the club, a man by the name of Mack Smith, came out talk to him. Mack stuffed a twenty-dollar bill in Regan's front shirt pocket. ack Smith proceeded to offer Regan a five-dollar tip for every customer he uld bring to the club. For the next few days, Regan struggled with the offer.

The following Sunday, after taking communion, Regan realized that even though he really needed the money, he could not commit that very mortal sin. After Mass, Regan went to the collection box in the back of the church, slipp the twenty-dollar bill into the slot, and let it fall. Eventually, Regan found a jol doing what he was trained to do in the Marines, working on airplanes.

Eiryanna continued to romanticize about her college years. In her heart, she longed to return to all the fantastic social events of sorority life. Eiryanna realized that she should have married a college professor. Eiryanna found no pleasure in domestic life, feeling trapped in its servile housekeeping duties. Li her mother before her, Mom trained all of us five kids how to do the house wor chores. Mom showed us how to wash dishes, how to properly clean a floor on our hands and knees with a brush and bucket, how to iron our uniforms, how tc sew on a button properly, and how to clean our rooms including our closets.

Women's Depression III

The Limbic System is a group of structures in the center of the human brain. The Limbic System is composed of several important areas, including; the amygdala, the hippocampus, the hypothalamus, and the basal ganglia (whi includes the substantia nigra and the cingulate gyrus). The limbic System is considered to be a person's _emotional brain._

The Prefrontal Cortex is a brain structure located in an entirely differer area from the Limbic System. It is immediately behind the bony structures of the forehead. Its neural structures form a three-dimensional grid. The Prefrontal Cortex has nine functions, of which logic generation is primary. T Prefrontal Cortex is considered to be a person's _logical brain._

Under stressful situations, blood flow increased in men's prefrontal cortex, indicating an increased logic response. Under similar stressful situations, blood flow increased in women's limbic System, indicating a heightened emotional response. In women, this stress response in the limbic System was stronger and lasted longer than men's prefrontal cortex stress response. This correlates with the historically observed differences between women's and men's overall behavior patterns. Women's Limbic System emotive dominance is thought to be one of the main reasons that women experience two times the prevalence of depression when compared to men. (25), (26), (27), (28).

Kids Stories 5

Life with my brothers in my sixth Summer was going pretty good. Mowing lawns had made us wealthy enough to buy cap guns, transistor radios, and, of course, lots of candy. Clementine, the wild cat that only my Dad could pet, had a litter, and each of us boys tamed a kitten of our own. My brothers, Simon, who was nine, and Ike, who was seven, started telling me the hard facts about school. School had been an obscure concept with no real interest on my part, until they told me that I was going to have to sit in a chair for at least seven hours a day. Horror began to flood my mind as I could barely last sitting through supper most nights.

My first day in first grade at the Catholic School was the longest day of my then very long life, and I hated every minute of it. Mine was a small class of only sixty kids. My brother Ike's class had seventy. My desk was steel and wood torture device with a hard, uncomfortable seat. The nun was a massive, angry, black-robed woman with a hardwood ruler always in her hand. That sharp-edged ruler landed on some area of your body with great force and frequently, even when you were only whispering.

The ABCs were the first mountain to climb as we learned to shape the letters correctly between ruler blows. We were forced to hold the pencil between our thumb and our pointer finger with the pencil resting on the second finger far knuckle. Ouch, Ok, Ok, I'll do it that way. And why on earth did anyone need big and small letters? They meant the same thing anyway; it seemed so utterly stupid. We were coerced into writing words; little ones at first then came bigger ones. I could say the words perfectly well, so why did I have to learn how to write them? And what was the big deal about spelling? Spelling Bees were obviously for girls.

The majority of my time in first grade was spent daydreaming on the battleships formed by the clouds floating in the sky outside the classroom windows. My mind would drift back endlessly to the freedom of the adventures of my lost youth. Knowing that I had been sentenced to twelve long years in this terrible prison produced elaborate schemes of escape into the wild blue yonder.

Finally, Monday, May 2, 1960, arrived, and I was ecstatic. I knew I had only three more weeks until Summer and then three whole months of absolute freedom. The scary black robbed nun stood up and, in a harsh voice, commanded that all students must turn in all of our ABCs and all our notebooks. What ABCs and What Notebooks? Turns out we had been instructed at the beginning of the year to write our ABCs two times a day, every school day, for the entire year. I never remembered hearing anything about finishing our phonics work books at home every night. Unbridled fear rose up in my heart! I was in deep, deep dukie! I was going to flunk first grade!

My parents were summoned to the school that very next evening to have a conference with the Principle and the angry black-robed nun. Upon the parents' return from that meeting, I was the recipient of a painful belt woopin from my Dad. The next three weeks of my life were spent in a small room next to the janitor's closet, doing my forgotten ABCs and finishing my phonics workbooks. I will be forever proud to proclaim from the highest mountaintop that I graduated first grade.

Kids Stories 6

The Summer after first grade seemed like it lasted forever! Life was again filled with endless adventures with my brothers. In the second grade, with a non-interactive teacher, I began to be reconciled to my loss of freedom. As the Fall progressed, I settled into doing school tasks, however reluctantly.

Somewhere in that Autumn, the concept of prayer became stuck in my ponderings. One evening, out of curiosity, I asked my mother, a lifelong Catholic, how do you pray? She looked puzzled as if taken by surprise and responded, "Well, I guess you just talk to God."

For the next several weeks, when I lay down at night before sleep enveloped my consciousness, I would talk forthrightly with God. The events of the day, mostly the discouragements of school, were the main topics of my articulation to God. Gradually, as my nightly chats with God continued, I became aware that He was actually listening, and these one-way expoundings became two-way conversations, yes, even discussions.

One evening, during my now usual talk with God, the overwhelming presence of His Almighty Being entered my bedroom. This was not a visual apparition but something much greater. I found myself in a heightened reality irrespective of time, place, and personal age. The wonderous presence of the God that created the entire universe enveloped me in His glory. The intense irresistible gravity of the all-encompassing love of Jesus was drawing me like iron to a magnet with a pull beyond measure. My heart responded to His caring warmth with a love so powerful it radiated throughout my entire self. Jesus began to show me what I was to look like physically and the person I was to be mentally in my adulthood.

The pagan He revealed me to be, was a wholly self-consumed rebel at war with all. A person who stood against every realm of authority, including God Himself. The distance between Jesus and myself was shown to be an unbridgeable chasm. This spiritual separation resembled a massive canyon of agony that no man could cross.

A deep sadness completely enveloped my soul as I realized the impossibility of any reconciliation. Somehow, I knew He was the King and that he had a glorious kingdom that was totally beyond my possible reach. In that eternal moment, I made a lifetime covenant with my creator. From the center of my being, I vouchsafed my life to Him. Whatever hardship, trial, or suffering H had to put me through in order to grant me passage into His kingdom, I was willing to walk through it. In that everlasting moment, He entered the Holy of Hollies of my heart, taking over every aspect of my existence. The ocean of His inexpressibly glory engulfed me with a wonderous joy.

Dianna I

On Monday, September 3, 1962, third grade began with my usual reluctance to return to school. Then suddenly everything changed when my new teacher, Mrs. Dianna Sterling, introduced herself. For the first time in my life, I encountered a woman who was beautiful both inside and out. Mrs. Sterling was a true Southern Lady without pretense. She possessed a brigh warm smile, loving eyes, and a gentle voice full of joy and compassion. She had a way of making you want to learn the lesson no matter how dull the subject matter seemed. All the kids were enraptured by Mrs. Sterling, and class became a fun time that everyone looked forward to.

My brothers and I had determined, a long time prior, that "Yes Sir," "No am," and all that polite stuff were for sissies. Hugs and kisses from females ere beyond terrible and not to be endured. If I skinned my elbow, going wild on e playground, I wore it like the medal of honor. Then, I would return to class oudly, strutting my badge of toughness.

Mrs. Sterling, upon seeing my red badge, would hurry over and survey my ound, gently clean and band-aid it. She would then proceed to give me a hug. he would say sicky-sweet things like, "Oh, you poor little darlin, does it hurt." ed with embarrassment, I would stammer and stutter, not knowing how to react. time, her hugs and affection became the wealth of my life.

Mrs. Sterling was a very innovative educator. She taught us all how to gure in our heads." She showed us how to break down addition, subtraction, ltiplication, and division into their simple component parts. Doing each aller function by itself, it became simple. Then, by rejoining the parts into a ole, the complex problem was instantly solved. With this mechanism, she ught us how to do math in our heads without paper or pencil.

She also taught us how to speed-read. The first task was to skip the ercise of pronouncing the word in our head. Then, by teaching our minds to cognize the meaning of words by sight, reading became simpler. Sentences uld suddenly convey their full energy. Paragraphs would encapsulate a finitive thought and action. Soon, we were flying through page after page, ught up in the author's mindset.

Mrs. Sterling taught us how to write. Nouns became bows, and verbs came arrows. Sentences became warriors, and paragraphs became armies. riting became a way to describe the battleships seen in the clouds of my ydreams. By focusing on the concept and letting the words flow, writing came an adventure in and of itself. With Mrs. Sterling leading the way, 100l was no longer something to be dreaded but the bicycle I could ride into a ure of promise.

Female Teachers

Teaching elementary school is an increasingly difficult task in a society where most parents no longer teach their children to lead a self-disciplined life. Teachers, therefore, must have a calling and a love for children. They must possess almost unlimited patience without an anger response to the anger expressed. They need a gentle and calm voice that allows the student to let down their guard. Teaching requires having a slow and soft touch, which gives the student time and confidence to begin learning the motions of writing and a Teachers need a bright and alive mood that coaxes the child out of their emotional shell to see that learning is fun. These are only a few of the traits a teacher needs to make them fully equipped to succeed in elementary education.

Yes, elementary teachers must be able to transfer knowledge from a boo into the child's mind. What is vastly more important, however, is to successfull encourage the child into each new level of the learning process. One aspect that elementary teachers enjoy is helping the child accept the discipline of learning as a joyful adventure. Then, the encouraged child begins to realize that this learning leads to the joy of fulfilling their dreams.

On average, women are principally driven by emotion. Due to this emoti drive, women tend to have a strong desire for warm personal relationships. Those wonderful relationships flourish in elementary school between the teacher and her students. Elementary school teachers almost invariably have favorite grade they love to teach. That particular age group is, to them, the perfect balance between openness and ability.

Children almost always develop a strong attachment to at least one teacher during their grade school years. Invariably, this was the teacher who took the time and put out the warmth to touch their hearts and open their min.

to the joy of learning. If this necessary encounter does not take place often times the child will resent the entire education process and will not embrace a lifetime of learning. (40), (41), (42).

Matthew 5;1: Jesus saw the crowds and went up on a hill, where he sat down. His disciples gathered round him, and he began to teach them.' NIV
Luke 5;1: One day as Jesus was standing by the Lake of Gennesaret with the people gathering around him listening to the word of God, he saw at the water's edge two boats, left there by the fishermen, who were washing their nets. He got into one of the boats, the one belonging to Simon, and asked him to put out a little way from shore. Then he sat down and taught the people from the boat.' NIV

Eiryanna XI

After all of her children were in Catholic Elementary School, Eiryanna took a job teaching the eighth grade at that same Catholic Elementary. During her first year, she met Dianna, who taught third grade, and they became fast friends. In her second year, her oldest son, Simon, was one of her students, and it was to her an answer to prayer. The other mothers soon began to raise a seemingly endless series of complaints due to their perception that she was showing favoritism towards her son. With three more children in the grades below, she could see that this would keep happening. Additionally, Eiryanna had to take into account that Catholic elementary school teacher salaries were terribly low and without benefits. Towards the end of that year, she came to the realization that the local university was her only option for moving ahead in her public school teaching ambitions.

Dianna II

Mrs. Sterling had a son two grades ahead of me. Jack was tall, intelligent, and very handsome, with wavey blond hair. He was an Adonis of a figure. The most singular trait about Jack was his unpretentious kindness. All the students held Jack in an awe, just short of worship.

In the sixth grade, I got all pumped up about football and decided to join the school team. It was fun and a place where I could vent all of my very energetic aggression without getting in trouble. The sixth graders did not get to play in the actual games, as we were there to learn the game during the practice sessions. Practice after practice, I was beginning to acquire the needed fundamental skills, from the three-point stance to blocking, to my favorite task, tackling. Being a very fast runner with exceptional agility and balance, I quickly learned how to get past the offensive front line and into the backfield. Once there, I would focus on tackling the quarterback or the running back. This resulted in the coach heaping praise on my abilities. However, it also resulted in the coach heaping derision on the eighth-grade offensive players I was able to outplay. This went on week after week.

Suffice to say, I soon became very unpopular with the eighth graders. Two of the eighth graders, Philip and John, both a head taller than I, developed a solution to the pesky sixth grader. They began to double-team me, clip me, helmet spike me, and in short trying their best to injure me. Somewhere around midseason, one of those clips succeeded in severely injuring my knee to the extent that I could no longer run, and I was benched. The knee did not get better, and I was reduced to hobbling around school with a rage against my enemies building in every part of my being.

One lunch period before the Friday game, I snuck into the practice shed, where all the players' equipment was stored. I found Philip and John's stuff and quickly proceeded to fill their cleated shoes with line-marker chalk. Sneaking back out, I went on my way with a hidden smile.

After having a wonderful weekend filled with the joy of revenge, Monday came back around. A very angry Phillip and John confronted me on the playground at lunch, loudly proclaiming their intent to pummel me into the ground. In the instant before the melee began, Jack Sterling inserted himself between the warring parties. With great force Jack confronted both boys and told them that they would have to fight him first. Pure fright lit up their countenances as they very quickly turned and walked away. Jack Sterling was a true hero of the noblest order.

Eiryanna XII

Eiryanna, with much encouragement from Dianna, enrolled in the local university that next Fall. University life set Eiryanna free. She became a consummate student, taking voluminous notes for every class and engaging in uplifting conversations with her professors. After four years of diligent study, she earned a Bachelor's Degree in English with a minor in History. She went on to get her teaching certification the following year. Feeling as though she was on top of the world, she set out to acquire her initial placement in the Public School System.

As the months went by, Eiryanna began to get discouraged as one rejection letter after another began to pile up on her old wooden desk at the house. Eiryanna could painfully see that in the hiring process, there was always a line of younger women ahead of her applying for each and every teaching position. Over time, she was forced to accept the hard reality that at forty-five years of age, no school was going to hire her.

Dianna III

Jack Sterling went on from the Catholic Grade School to the local Catholic High School. Jack excelled in high school, graduating with honors. Jack was accepted at the top state university in the capital city. In college, Jack not only excelled in his academic studies but was also very popular in college social circles. Jack was elected president of his class and led his class with great industry and enthusiasm. During this time period, a large portion of his age group was caught up in the abject hedonism of the hippy movement. As a true leader, Jack had the courage to vocally confront this dissipation and proclaim his allegiance to Christ. After graduating summa cum laude at the university, Jack was accepted to a very prestigious Law School.

During law school, Jack became engaged and then married the love of his life. Despite the rigors of Law School and the challenges of a new marriage, Jack continued to be active in his church. Jack graduated from Law School summa cum laude and was hired by one of the most prominent law firms in the country. Life for Jack Sterling, at this juncture, was filled with unlimited hope and promise.

About a year after joining the law firm, Jack's workload became extreme. Jack, however, kept his shoulder to the plow and did not complain. During that year, he began to lose weight and experience persistent fatigue. He wrote it off as the workload. Gradually, at first, but then with increasing frequency, he started having nose bleeds. Then tiny red spots began appearing on his arms and legs.

Jack happened to mention all of this during a phone call with his mother, Dianna. Dianna insisted that he go to the doctor at once, but Jack refused, stating that he had to finish a pretrial motion for a very important case. Dianna drove to the capital city and made an appointment for Jack with an Internal Medicine Specialist.

That evening, Dianna, together with Jack's wife, had a knockdown, drag out confrontation with Jack when he arrived home from the office, late.

hat next Monday morning, with great reluctance, Jack went to a doctor's ffice for the first time in his adult life. He told the doctor that he had simply en working too much and had gotten some sort of cold. Jack allowed the ctor to do all the exams and blood work that he didn't consider really cessary, just to satisfy his wife and his mother. Jack went from the doctor's ffice straight to work, frustrated that he was now really behind on that pretrial tion.

Weeks went by, and Jack's symptoms persisted. One morning, he got a ll from the Internist who insisted that he and his wife absolutely must be at the ctor's office no later than nine am that very next day. The following morning, t of duty, a relaxed Jack and his very worried wife were seated in the private ffice of the Internist. Jack kept reassuring his wife that he was sure that it was ally nothing more than a nagging cold.

The Internist entered the office with a file in his hand and a somber look on face. He then shook both Jack and his wife's hands. The Internist sat wn at his desk and began reading lab results foreign to Jack's understanding. he Internist stopped for a very tense moment, looked Jack straight in the eye, d told Jack that he had a very rare and difficult-to-treat form of Leukemia. he Internist reassured Jack and his then-sobbing wife that he was going to do very level best to see to it that Jack survived. Within a year, despite eiving the best cancer treatment available, Jack Sterling died.

Genetics IV

Across virtually every type of cancer, occurrence rates are higher in males an females. In some cancers, the incidence is two to three times higher in males. certain individuals, the cancer-fighting cells formed by a gene labeled DM6A located on the X sex chromosome carry a mutation that disables em. KDM6A has only one active copy on the solo male X sex chromosome. owever, KDM6A escapes inactivation on the (not so silent) female X sex chromosome, giving the female two active copies. This added protection is thought to be one reason why there are significantly lower cancer rates in females. (43).

Dianna IV

At the grave, Dianna could not hear the priest's words due to a persistent bussing and clanging in her ears. Not just her eyes but every part her being seemed to be weeping in a monsoon of bitterness. After the grave back at her house, people's voices were heard only as muffled noises of incoherent mumblings. For weeks, she sat in a chair, barely able to drink wate or swallow any sustenance.

Then, the bitterness within her soul began to darken and deepen. He mind became obsessed with ways of ending the misery. First softly and infrequently, then with increasing stridency and rage, she began to call out, "Why, Lord." She began to scream at God with every fiber of her being, begging to die because she did not want to live in a world without her beloved son.

Months went by inside her house without Dianna caring or even knowi what was going on in the forsaken world outside. Dianna became lost onto t world. The pills helped her get a little broken sleep. In her dreams she wandered through marish nights of lost groping through darkened caves fille with constant unbearable pain. Days were spent in shuttered rooms, lighting one cigarette off the last, staring at the meaningless patterns in the wallpape Finally, she arrived at the end goal of her plan. She had saved up enough o her sleeping pills to put an end to this hopeless life of endless misery.

In the moment before she took the first pill, the tiniest pinpoint of a beguiling white light appeared in her room of torment. Slowly but steadily, t light became larger and brighter. With the light came a flood of peace that began to extinguish all of her incurable pain. The light and its peace soon invaded every corner of her existence. Then, a voice sweeter and more lovely than any she had ever witnessed spoke into her frozen heart. I am the Ancient of Days, and today, I bring the mercy and salvation of my son Jesus that you may be restored to all joy. Dianna bathed in that heavenly white light for what seemed like an eternity. Without volition, her hand spontaneously reached over to the side table and placed the bible on her lap. It fell open, and she read;

"He had no beauty or majesty to attract us to Him, nothing in his appearance that we should desire Him. He was despised and rejected by men, a man of sorrows and familiar with suffering. Like one from whom men hide their faces. He was despised, and we esteemed him not. Surely, he took up our infirmities and carried our sorrows, yet we considered him stricken by God, smitten by Him, and afflicted. But He was pierced for our transgressions, He was crushed for our iniquities; the punishment that brought us peace was upon Him, and by His wounds we are healed." Isaiah 53;2: NIV

Gradually, Dianna began to move back into the flow of life. She joined a Pentecostal Bible study, where the group was beginning a treatment of 'Acts.' She became very curious about 'The Baptism of the Holy Spirit.' It scared her and yet, at the same time, intrigued her. She read every book she could find on it. One night, while deep in prayer, she felt a warmth in her heart. Immediately, she began to pray out loud in strange utterances. Somehow, she remembered the words of her unknown prayer and wrote them down. After diligently searching for months, she discovered, to her amazement, that she had prayed the 'Our Father' in Mandarin Chinese.

The Grief of a Lost Child

Grief is a natural human emotion that occurs when an individual experiences the death of a loved one. The person is enveloped in and permeated by an overwhelming sadness and a sense of irreconcilable loss. This period of mourning can last for many months. The symptoms of grief can look a lot like depression. However, grief is almost always associated with a one-time event of the loss of someone of great value in a person's life. Grief is a natural response that tends to dissipate over time. Grief normally presents in fairly typical stages.

In the immediate time period following the loss, oftentimes, the person goes into shock and then denial. The individual in shock has difficulty even fully processing what has happened. They will often go into denial and verbalize something on the order of "this can't be happening." As the person begins to further process the event, women tend to react with uncontrollable crying, and men tend to respond with red-hot anger. The grieved can then fall into a false bargaining process that presents as a promise to cease a particular behavior if the situation would only reverse itself. When the realization sets in that no change in themselves can change the outcome of the event, intense sadness sets in.

As time passes, the grieved person begins to accept the hard reality of the loss. Many describe this recognition as "the lifting of a fog." As acceptance progresses, sadness lessens, and the individual gains perspective on their loss. It is common in this phase for the grieved to remember the good times they spent with the person they have lost. (44).

Takotsubo Syndrome (TTS), also known as "broken heart syndrome," is characterized by a sudden temporary weakening of the heart muscles. This muscle weakness causes the left ventricle to balloon out at the bottom while the neck remains narrow. Evidence indicates that TTS is typically triggered by episodes of severe emotional distress following the loss of a loved one. TTS is more common in women, with only ten percent of the cases occurring in men. (45).

With deep disappointment, verging on outright anger, Eiryanna had to let go of her dream of becoming a teacher in the Public Schools. Having been a social worker during the war, a field she was not all that fond of, she began applying for employment in social work. After a long and laborious search, she found a job in Houston, doing what she had done in San Deigo, an Inspector of daycare centers.

What she found in these centers shocked her: hot rooms with dirt and trash on the floor, unwashed children with soiled diapers, poorly prepared meals on unwashed plates with no spoons or other utensils, and old broken toys that were a hazard to the children.

Eiryanna became determined to transform these centers into environments that were clean and safe for the children. With her Yankee work ethic invigorated, she put her shoulder to the plow. In time, the centers she inspected became the best in the Houston area. The parents and her supervisors began to take notice. Eiryanna was elevated to the position of Superintendent of daycare licensing, with the duty of teaching new hires. She taught her new recruits how to make the centers compliant with the codes. Moreover, Eiryanna trained her inspectors to inspire the owners and managers of the daycare centers to transform their facilities into harbors of beauty and joy that would be beneficial for the children.

Now in her late fifties, Eiryanna was offered a position as Director of Daycare Licensing in a county west of Harris County. The position came with a substantial increase in salary and stature. Eiryanna, after much prayer, accepted. After all the wonderful welcomes and fanfare had subsided, Eiryanna decided to begin visiting the centers unannounced.

The centers were as bad or worse than the Houston area centers were when she first started. Additionally, after interviewing the directors of these centers, she discovered that the county inspectors were simply doing short, five-to-ten-minute walk-throughs. The Directors revealed they had not received any follow-up recommendations for improvements after the visits. When she returned to her office, hot under the collar, she began to rummage through all her files, looking for the notes of her employee's past visits. What she found were barely legible short scribblings that described the various centers as fully compliant with no recommendations for improvement.

The following Friday, Eiryanna canceled all Monday center visits and called a Monday morning must-show meeting at eight am sharp for all of her subordinates. In that meeting, Eiryanna laid down the law. Each inspector would be required to visit one center a day, and the initial visit would last a minimum of five hours. During that visit, a list of ten major areas of concern must be inspected and graded. Upon returning to the office, a typed report must be completed and turned in by the end of the day. In that report, all ten areas of concern must be addressed, describing the state of those areas in full. Then, a list of deficiencies and detailed recommendations must be created to correct any deficiencies found during the visit. The list of deficiencies and recommendations would be mailed to the Daycare Owners Director.

Within a month, the inspector would return to the center. The inspector must physically tour the areas of concern, showing the Director the deficiencies and explaining exactly what must be done to correct the problems. Regular return visits would be required to regrade the center and add new recommendations if needed.

Her employees were silent and sat slack-jawed after Eiryanna had finished her inquisition. As they filed slowly out of the room, they were each handed a ring binder containing a thick list of requirements for each visit. Over the coming weeks and months, most of the inspectors reluctantly complied with the new paradigm. Those who did not comply and ignored her mandates were summarily fired, and new inspectors were hired. Over the course of the next year, Eiryanna continued to make unannounced visits to the centers under her ontrol, and she saw substantial improvement in all of the areas of concern. However, most of Eiryanna's staff were distant and hostile just below the urface.

In the second year of her directorship, the parents who used the centers egan to take notice of the substantial improvements. Through a flood of tters, the parents made the County Commissioners well aware of their pproval of Eiryanna's leadership. Eiryanna received an award plaque at the nnual County Fair Dinner for excellence in service to the County. Feeling at she had finally reached a place of appreciation for all of her hard work, iryanna was finally at peace with the direction her life had taken.

Empathy Women II

Since the Great Greek Writers first put feather pen to parchment, it has een observed that women possess greater empathy than men. Empathy has o components; cognitive empathy and affective empathy. Cognitive empathy defined as the ability to recognize another person's thoughts and feelings. ognitive empathy is a fundamental part of human social interaction and ommunication because it is the first necessary step in putting ourselves in the her person's shoes. Females have a significantly higher ability to read the notions displayed in another person's facial expressions. Affective empathy is e ability to respond with an appropriate emotion to someone else's perceived oughts and feelings. (21), (22), (23), (24).

Eiryanna XIV

Eiryanna arrived at work one Monday morning several months after ceiving her award, and to her surprise, none of the employees were present. here was a letter fixed with scotch tape to her desk. Upon opening and reading the letter, she was in profound shock. The letter stated that all of her employees were on strike and would remain so until she was removed from her post. It was signed by each and every one of her staff. The County Commissioners were also given the same letter.

After much consternation and heated argument, a majority of the Commissioners voted to offer Eiryanna early retirement. Eiryanna, with great reluctance, submitted her resignation. Eiryanna, although deeply wounded, held her head high, knowing that the most important people in the entire situation were the children. She knew that due to her uncompromising leadership, these children were now in daycare centers where their lives were vastly improved.

Eiryanna was very active in retirement, attending bible studies and visiting the friends she had made over the years. She mostly loved to sit at the table her well-appointed kitchen and read. She kept the windows tightly shut to eliminate noise. The house next door was occupied by less than fastidious people and was full of various bugs. Eiryanna would have her house sprayed monthly to keep it bug-free. When you walked into her home, you were immediately aware of the strong odor of bug spray. Most of these pesticides contain a chemical that kills roaches, which is a type of nerve poison.

Pesticide Neurologic Effects

Mounting evidence over the past several decades shows that chronic exposure to low levels of pesticides adversely affects the Central Nervous System (CNS). Pesticide exposure can impact a plethora of neurological disorders, including but not limited to Amyotrophic Lateral Sclerosis (ALS Parkinson's disease, Alzheimer's, and Progressive Supranuclear Palsy. Long term low-dose exposure to pyrethroids (a main ingredient in roach spray) can induce oxidative stress, mitochondrial dysfunction, synuclein fibrillization, and tau formation (found in PSP), leading to neuronal cell death. Organophosphates have also been shown to lead to tau formation. (46)

Regan III

Regan refused to retire and continued as a shift worker in an aircraft assembly plant. Due to the disappearance of his own father when he was ten, Regan's greatest ambition was to be a great father. His overwhelming disappointment in the 'hippie' lifestyle his children had taken left him feeling that he had failed as a father. During the years his kids were in the home Regan had been a weekend beer drinker. However, now that the children were grown and gone, Regan slowly fell into excessive daily alcohol consumption. The Elks Club became his steady haunt. A shot of Canadian Club with a cold Budweiser to follow, known as 'a boiler maker and a helper,' was his oft-repeated call. At eleven thirty every evening, he would climb into his dated Cadilac and drive the two miles from the Elks Club to the house, then go straight to bed.

Alcohol Addiction

Women are four times less likely to be afflicted with alcoholism than men. Many thousands of people die every year from alcohol-related deaths; one-third of these are women. Around 46 percent of all adult women and 58 percent of all adult men drink alcohol on a regular basis. Approximately 10 percent of women and 25 percent of men engage in binge drinking. About 10 percent of pregnant women drink alcohol. Excessive drinking may disrupt a woman's menstrual cycle and increase the risk of infertility. Women are more vulnerable than men to the brain-damaging effects of excessive alcohol use.

Women who drink excessively are at a greater risk for heart damage than men. Even moderate drinking over several decades increases the risk of dementia to around sixty percent after the sixtieth year. Alcohol decreases brain cells' ability to change voltage.

The release of dopamine, the brain's "feel-good" neurotransmitter, is a significant factor in alcoholism. Men produce more dopamine while drinking, which reinforces continued drinking. Alcohol has several known primary targets in the body. These are the NMDA, GABA, and nACh receptors, as well as $Ca2+$ channels and $K+$ channels. Following the first hit of alcohol on specific targets in the brain, a second wave of indirect effects on a variety of neurotransmitter/neuropeptide systems is initiated. This second wave leads to the typical acute behavioral effects of alcohol, ranging from disinhibition to sedation. The first by-product generated during alcohol metabolism, Acetaldehyde, can affect the activity of different neurotransmitter systems and, subsequently, can contribute to the behavioral effects of alcohol. (47).

Dianna V

Over the years, when I would return to my hometown for visits with my folks, I would drop by and visit Dianna at her home. At this stage, in her eighty-plus-year life, Dianna exhibited the expected effects of aging. Her face was wrinkled, her body bent over, and she walked with a slow, unsteady gait.

However, as you entered Dianna's presence, you encountered a very exclusive phenomenon. There was subtle enhancement of the radiance of the light surrounding her. The colors were more brilliant, the hues were more pleasant to the eye, and the dimensions possessed an ever so slightly spherical quality. Her smile, as warm and beautiful as in her youth, now radiated the tender love of the eternal God. Dianna had grown so close to her loving Creator that she radiated the very presence of Jesus Christ.

Eiryanna XV

Eiryanna endured her alcoholic husband for many years until the silence became deafening. She, again and again, demanded that he seek treatment and get sober. Finally, tired of all the nagging, Regan entered a treatment program and two weeks later emerged sober. Regan was sober for about five months, then slipped back into his drinking. After enduring his drinking for another year, she demanded that he go back to treatment, or she would leave. Regan went back into treatment, but his sobriety only lasted three months this time.

Eiryanna rented a small apartment across town. She contracted a moving company and moved out in one day. Tired of all the nagging at this point, Regan was glad to see her go. After several months of drunken solitude, Regan heard the doorbell ring early one Saturday morning. The polite man at the door served him with divorce papers. Regan went to the frig and got a can of cold Budweiser, popped the top, then sat down in his comfortable old chair. As he sipped his beer, he read the divorce papers. Out of the corner of his eye, Regan caught the glint of an old Rosary hanging from a lamp on the coffee table. He shuffled over and lifted it up. For the first time since his father had left, all those years ago, Regan began to pray the Rosary.

Later that day, Regan went to confession. The next day, Sunday, Regan went to communion, and on Monday, he went back into rehab. This time, Regan went into rehab with a resolve that only his newly reestablished relationship with his Savior could provide. After a month of rehab, Regan emerged as a truly changed man and never went back to the bottle.

Divorce

It has always been presumed that couples who fought the least had the longest and most stable marriages. However, studies have shown that the absence or presence of quarrels had little effect on marital longevity. What ha been discovered is that couples who had a long-term friendship before the romance blossomed had the highest probability of a successful long-term marriage. This is due to the reality that romance is a rollercoaster ride with incredible highs and low lows. During the lows of romance, the bond of friendship strengthens and preserves the marital relationship.

Women initiate three-quarters of all divorces. Perhaps this is due to the reality that married women reported lower levels of relationship quality than married men. One of the most significant factors in long-term marital stability and satisfaction is a couple's kindness toward each other on a daily basis. Couples who consistently express appreciation and interest in each other for stronger bonds of intimacy. Relational generosity in marriage is a very healing factor. The reality of mutual positive regard heals the daily woundings that ar part of the marital struggle. (48).

Dianna VI

When I was in the early years of my medical practice in a far-off town, I got a call from my mother, Eiryanna. Mom told me that Dianna had been diagnosed with late-stage rapidly advancing lung cancer. A cloud of melancho hung over my heart for many days after that. My mind recalled the sweet days of my youth when Dianna poured her unbridled love into my soul and her infectious enthusiasm for the future into my mind. Slowly, joy began to creep back into my thought life as I realized she was going home to be with her Savio Jesus Christ and with Jack, the son that she constantly missed.

My dislike for funerals had always been rooted in the fact that they, for some reason, seemed to occur three days too late. By the time of the actual ceremony, the spirit of the departed person is either in the Kingdom of God c

omewhere else. It seemed appropriate for Dianna that a bon voyage party was
 order. This send-off party must include all of the many people she had
essed over the years of her teaching career.

     After forty years of disconnect, even putting together a complete phone
st of fellow students was a herculean task. A short list eventually came
gether, as many of my third-grade class still lived in my hometown. The guys I
as able to get a hold of were very concerned about Dianna and were gung-ho
r the party idea. They called others, and those others called others, and in
ort order, we had a team.

     When I called the Catholic Parish, Monsignor Phillip, from the football
ars, picked up the phone. He was already well aware of Dianna's situation
d volunteered the old church building as a place for the event. By the
tlandish grace of God, the party came off miraculously. Scores of former
udents from every decade of her teaching years were in attendance. With
iles on all their faces, tears in all their eyes, and oceans of love in all their
arts, they all came to wish Dianna Sterling the very best of goodbyes.
nce in a lifetime, you might get lucky and be blessed enough to have a person
e Dianna involved in your formative years. Saints are not photographs of
inted statues with wired on halos, printed upon stiff paper cards. Saints are
ry real people, totally given to God, in a very fallen world. Dianna, with a
yful smile on her face, died ten days after her party. Her soul was carried into
aven by a band of mighty angels. Dianna went forever to be with her son,
ack, in the glorious presence of her Lord and Savior, Jesus Christ.

ReganIV

     After his return to work at the factory Regan began a program of daily
alks to restore his health. Regan was determined to get back to a vigorous,
aningful life after so many years of dissipation. The walks, however, began

to be limited by severe chest pain. A stress test and then an Arteriogram wer[e]
done at the doctor's office. Several days later, the Cardiologist called Rega[n]
into his office and told him he needed to have Coronary Artery Bypass
Surgery. Never one to avoid life, Regan went into the hospital a week later h[ad]
the surgery done. It took many months for Regan to get back to his walking.
Eiryanna had never followed through on the divorce. After Regan had been
sober for an entire year and after many months of joint counseling, Eiryanna
moved back into the house. By the renewing grace of God, Eiryanna and
Regan managed to rekindle their romance.

Pragma;
Love Based on Maturity and Commitment.

Eiryanna XVI

In her mid-eighties, Eiryanna began to experience difficulty keeping her
balance. At first, she was resistant to using a cane but did so after much
prodding. Eventually, her ever-increasing problem of keeping her balance whi[le]
walking led to her having to use a walker, which Eiryanna really hated. Eiryan[na]
went to all sorts of medical specialists without getting a definitive diagnosis.
Finally, after a series of MRI imaging studies, it was determined that she had [a]
disease known as Progressive Supranuclear Palsy (PSP). This neurologica[l]
pathology pertained to the denigration of the motor neurons of the limbs (call[ed]
the homunculus) located on the side of the brain above the ear canals. As th[e]
name Progressive indicates, it had a history of worsening, and regrettably, the[re]
were no viable treatment options.

Regan became Eiryanna's caretaker as the disease worsened. Regan
took on the task of what he jokingly would refer to as "The chief cook and
bottle washer." Regan, now retired, became Eiryanna's 'anything that needs [

get done around the house' guy with a new joy brought on by his renewed faith in Christ. At this juncture, they could still do a bit of road traveling. Their favorite destination was Galveston, Texas. Only an hour's drive down the road, Galveston had a beautiful beach on the Gulf of Mexico. They would sit on the beach for long hours in folding chairs and talk.

Human Romantic Love III

Human romantic love pathways are also involved in altruism in general. In a society that highly values youth, beauty, and ability, often overlooked are some of the more important reasons that people bond. One of these very vital bonding reasons is taking care of each other into old age. Altruism is deeply rooted in our neural and genetic framework. Altruism motivates people to care for others when those others can no longer take care of themselves (29), (30), (31), (32), (33), (34), (35).

Eiryanna XVII

Within two years of the onset of the first PSP symptoms, Eiryanna lost the ability to walk and became confined to a wheelchair. Eiryanna took it in stride, but Regan was heartbroken as he constantly prayed for a cure. Despite his profound disappointment, Regan shouldered the increased burden like the tough Marine he was. Eventually Eiryanna lost her ability to stand and became confined to a bed. This necessitated that Regan, now in his eighties, to acquire a hydraulic hoist to change Eiryanna's diapers. Eiryanna's arm movement and hand dexterity were the next loss. Regan had to spoon-feed the wife he loved. Then, Eiryanna began to lose the ability to chew and swallow. After much heartbreak and consultation with her physicians, Regan scheduled to have a feeding tube surgically installed.

Regan was determined not to put Eiryanna in a nursing home as long as he could adequately care for her. Eiryanna's health continued to decline. She went into flexor contracture and could only whisper. At this point, due to the ardent insistence of her children and her Doctors, Regan put Eiryanna on hospice.

Several weeks later, after a very contentious yelling match with one of his sons and with much personal sorrow, Regan signed a DNR. That evening, with tears streaming down his cheeks, Regan went into her room to see Eiryanna. Smiling, she motioned for him to come close with her eyes. Barely able to move her lips, Eiryanna whispered sweetly, "The best decision I ever made was to marry you, my cherished Regan; you are the love of my life." With that, Eiryanna breathed her last. Three and a half years after the onset of Progressive Supranuclear Palsy, Eiryanna, fully mentally aware, died. Eiryanna was joyful in death as she knew that she going home to be with her beloved Lord and Savior, Jesus Christ.

Progressive Supranuclear Palsy

Progressive Supranuclear Palsy is a rare neurological disorder that degrades many functional abilities, including body movements, balance during walking, and eye movements. PSP is believed to be caused by damage to motor neurons in the brain. It is an atypical parkinsonism in the category of frontotemporal disorders. PSP typically begins in the mid-to-late sixties and usually worsens rapidly into severe disability within three to five years.

The most frequent first symptom of PSP is loss of balance while ambulating, leading to falls that can leave the individual disabled. Stiffness and slow movement can also be seen in the first phase. As PSP progresses, eye and vision disorders begin to develop. Then, additional changes become noticeable, including mask-like facial non-expressiveness, difficulty sleeping for extended periods, slurred speech, forgetfulness, and lack of motivation.

A signature of PSP is the accumulation of the protein Tau in brain areas. The Tau accumulation is evidenced in the substantia nigra, a structure that is part of the limbic system thought to be the brain's emotional center. The Tau accumulation can also be seen in the motor neurons that power the body's musculature, causing eventual loss of body movement.

The exact cause of PSP is unknown. However, exposure to toxic chemicals is suspected due to the increase of these chemicals in the modern household environment. There is currently no effective treatment for reversing or delaying PSP. (49)

Greek Philosophy:

The Subjective / Objective Divide

About one hundred years before the death of Socrates, a dispute, indeed an argument, arose between two Greek philosophers, Heraclitus and Parmenides. Heraclitus believed the primary pathway to truth was through the five senses (objective/inductive). His foundational saying was, "No man steps in the same river twice." He viewed the world as constantly in flux, always becoming but never being complete, always on the road but never arriving at the destination.

Parmenides believed that the primary pathway to truth begins in the mind (subjective/deductive). Parmenides exposed the belief that what is changing in the material realm (diversity) has unity in the formal realm. Parmenides viewed the constantly changing world as simply the external appearance of a single unseen, unchanging, eternal substance that gives all things have unity. These two thinkers stumbled onto the great, seeming unbridgeable divide in all thought known as the 'Subjective / Objective Divide.' All esteemed philosophers from that time forward struggled at some point to bridge that divide.

Aristotle, the great student of Pato, sought to unify the subjective and the objective with his theory of 'Substance.' Aristotle reasoned that every Substance (except one) was composed of two parts; Mater and Form. The Material is what we perceive with our five senses and is ever-changing. The Formal is what we cannot perceive, never changes, and gives unity to all things. Aristotle reasoned that a Substance cannot be pure Mater, as without Form (beinghood), existence is not possible. However, Aristotle further delineated that there is one Substance that is composed of pure Form. This Substance containing only pure Form defined Aristotle's concept of a non-personal god. Additionally, Aristotle named the superficial exterior presentation of a substance, Accidens.

From a purely motor response (muscle movement) perspective, when we experience an action that is new to our personal history, our visual cortex relay information to our parietal cortex. Then, that information is passed on to our premotor memory. This relay of sensual input to our premotor memory then informs the motor neurons how to control our muscle movements to respond to the new situation.

However, when we experience an action that we ourselves have previous performed, such as riding a bicycle, an additional process takes place. The known event causes information to begin to flow in two directions. In the forward direction, our visual cortex relays information to our parietal cortex, which is then passed on to our premotor memory. In the reverse direction, information begins to flow from the premotor memory, to the parietal cortex, to the visual cortex. Therefore, we are effectively experiencing present sensory (objective) input and memory (subjective) input in the exact same time frame. This two-way information relay bridges the subjective/objective divide, allowin both a learned response and new input to be utilized to effectively improve our motor response to the immediate event.

From the emotional standpoint, when people see an incident (in the present
alm) that is similar to an emotion stirring event in their past several inductive
d deductive flows join in confluence. The present visual input evokes a
esent emotional response in real-time. Then, a remembered emotion caused
the similar past event resurfaces. Both of these emotions join and begin to
od the mind. Then, both of these subjective emotional forces inform the
esent objective input, adding color and wisdom of response to the present
cident that the person is experiencing. Therefore, our perception of present
ents in objective reality is almost always in some way influenced by our
bjective, emotive thought and our subjective, emotive memory. (51)

Limits of Perception

Our five senses by which we perceive the hard, objective reality of the
tside world are very limited at best. The portion of the rainbow of the
ctromagnetic radiation spectrum that is observable to the human eye is only
out 0.0035 percent. We can only see so far into the distance and so far into
e minuscule. Humans, on average, cannot hear sounds with a frequency less
an 20 Hz or sounds with a frequency greater than 20,000 Hz. Touch, smell,
d taste have similar limitations. As we age, even these very limited sensory
rceptions become more and more degraded and, in many cases, cease to
nction entirely.

Two earnest believers read the same scripture verse and come away with
o very different understandings. Why? The word of God is
comprehensible. Human logic is linear, from point A, to point B, to point C.
od's logic can be thought of as spherical or perhaps as supra-logical, as it is
far above human logic. Due to their limited logical ability, the believer can
prehend the meaning of scripture but never fully comprehend it. We are only
en a handful, and every believer is given a significantly different handful. Just

like our senses, our minds are limited in scope, and each mind has different limitations of scope.

2Kg 6: 17: " *Then the Lord opened the servant's eyes, and he looked, and the hills were full of horses and chariots of fire all around Elisha.*" NIV

Our ability to perceive in the spiritual realm is even more limited than our physical sensory perception and our logical mental perception. Those chariot of fire had been there all along, but the servant's spiritual eyes had been close So it is in our own lives, there are spiritual realities present in many instances; however, God has purposely limited our spiritual eyes' ability to perceive them We conduct our lives in a tiny village of physical, mental, and spiritual experien hemmed in by a wall of invisible darkness. On the outside of that wall, in real time, exists a megatropolis of physical, mental, and spiritual experience we have yet to be given the grace to perceive.

Taking Sides

One major trend stands out when undertaking an inquiry into new emerging positional movements that challenge prior well-established political, theological, and/or philosophical structures. The new movement always goes the completely opposite pole with a staunch repudiation of the thought proce that it is attempting to replace. When Communism is imposed upon a populac anything that is deemed tainted with the evils of Capitalism is quickly outlawe and discarded.

When the women's movement began, it was truly justified due to the reality that women were, in many cases, hindered from becoming all that God had called them to be. This was especially true if they felt led to pursue a traditionally male occupation. There is nothing unbiblical about a woman becoming a physician or a CEO of a large corporation. However, like all humanistic revolutions, the thought processes very quickly went to the opposite pole. Women, gifted with a servant's heart, who preferred to live out their spiritually superior life-giving role of motherhood and family were castigated by the Feminists as cowardly throwbacks.

The Servants Heart

At the Last Supper, Jesus gave a material example of what a servant's heart is to look like. Jesus took the posture of a servant to teach the apostles servanthood. Included in that group that Jesus washed the feet of was Judas. Jesus knew that Judas was preparing to betray Him.

John 13;4: "He got up from the meal, took off his outer cloak, and wrapped a towel around his waist. After that, He poured water into a basin and began to wash His disciple's feet, drying them with the towel." NIV

John 13;26: "Then dipping the piece of bread, He gave it to Judas Iscariot, son of Simon. As soon as Judas took the bread, Satan entered into him." NIV

Phil 2;6: "Who, being in very nature God, did not consider equality with God something to be grasped (held on to), but made Himself nothing, taking the very nature of a servant, being made in human likeness, and being found in appearance as a man, He humbled Himself and became obedient to death – even death on a cross!" NIV

Mat 20;26; "You know that the rulers of the Gentiles lord it over them, and their high officials exercise authority over them. Not so with you. Instead, whoever wants to become great among you must be your servant, and whoever wants to be first must be your slave. Just as the Son of Man did not come to be served, but to serve, and to give His life as a ransom for many." NIV

1 Peter 5;5: "All of you, clothe yourselves with humility toward one another, because, "God opposes the proud but gives grace to the humble." Humble yourselves, therefore, under God's mighty hand, that he may lift you up in due time." NIV

From a biblical perspective, men are given the role of leading through servanthood. However, there is a common observable duplicitousness in most men's leadership. They make the pretext that they are serving when, in reality, they are lording it over those under their authority. Before the East-West Schism in 1054 ad, there was one Christian church. From that time forward until the Reformation, there were two churches. At present, there are over forty thousand different non-denominational denominations worldwide.

Invariably, when a church splits, both sides zealously proclaim that they are the genuine holders of the true essential Christian Doctrine. In reality, church splits are primarily due to prideful men seeking to gain a following for themselves. Women see this double-minded attitude in men and become rightfully indignant. Pride is the final and the most difficult of all sins to overcome. "Power corrupts, and absolute power corrupts absolutely." The unbelieving world is totally consumed with the sin of pride. God's chosen people, His church, also struggle with pride.

Atheistic Existentialism; The Gospel of Death

The 'watershed' of all thought is the determination as to whether what we experience in this present world is an accidental illusion or a designed reality. The atheistic existentialist worldview assumes that what humans are encountering is an accidental discordant cacophony. If all is accidental, then Fredrich Niche was absolutely correct in concluding that everything we experience in the present realm is meaningless because accidents are

eaningless events. Fredrich Niche spent the last eleven years of his life in an
sane asylum, proclaiming himself to be Jesus Christ.

On that note, Bertrand Russell was indeed a visionary when he
etermined that we must accept "unrelenting despair" as a condition of true
nowledge. Going further in this accidental assumption, Albert Camu
orrectly stated the end game. Camu proclaimed that the only thing we
urselves get to determine is the 'nature and hour of our death.' Thus, Camu
dvocated suicide. Earnest Hemmingway, the renowned existentialist writer,
ook full advantage of this newfound freedom and willingly destroyed his own
xistence.

In the atheistic existential thought process, the individual nonchalantly
trolls on a wide, meandering downhill pathway to perdition. The harrowing
ileposts along this modern Broadway progressively degenerate from
ccidental, to vain meaninglessness, to unrelenting despair, to suicide.

The Gospel of Life

The other side of the watershed of thought describes a designed universe.
he acceptance of God's unfathomable design gives profound meaningfulness
 life. This meaningfulness unleashes abounding joy as opposed to
nrelenting despair. This abounding joy makes a person's life of immense value,
nd opposes life's willful demise in suicide.

It is crucial at this juncture to understand, succinctly, what the 'Gospel of
ife' is all about. The word 'Gospel' means the good news. The good news is
at the long-awaited Messiah, Jesus, has arrived as the Great Shepard. He,
nly, is the narrow door through which people must pass in order to enter into
e Kingdom of God.

The eternal, all-knowing, all-powerful God who created the entire
niverse left the perfect Kingdom of Heaven and became materially manifest in
 fallen world. He humbled Himself by becoming both the likeness and essence

of a human being in order to reconcile humanity to Himself. This God/Human, Jesus, was immaculately conceived by the Holy Spirit in the womb of virgin, Mary. This loving God entered the material world as the baby Jesus in the humblest circumstances. Jesus was born into and lived an ordinary working class, yet sinless life. Jesus, this sinless God/Human, was crucified on a cross bearing the weight of the sins of the entire human race. By the shedding of His blood on the cross, Jesus substitutionally paid the price for all the sins ever committed, enabling our personal Justification before God.

On the third day, Jesus rose from the dead, conquering death, enabling eternal life for all those who believe. Jesus ascended into heaven to be crowned 'King of Kings and Lord of Lords'. Jesus sits at the right hand of God the Father as the only 'High Priest' to make exclusive intercession for all believers.

1 Tim 2;5: "For there is one God and one mediator between God and men, Christ Jesus, who gave himself as a ransom for all men." (wo-men are included in 'all men'). NIV

Restoration of the Sacred

St Augustine was quoted as saying, "The New Testament is hidden in the Old Testament, and the Old Testament is revealed in the New Testament. From His Immaculate Conception, to His humble birth, to His Baptism by John, to the Last Supper, to His Death on the Cross, to His Resurrection from the Dead, to His Ascension into heaven, the life of Jesus was both a completion and a beginning. The total life of Jesus fulfilled, completed, and finished the Old Covenant of the law of Sin and Death. In that same life, Jesus began and gave Substance to the New Covenant of Life in the Spirit.

Salvation; Subjective
The Sovereignty of God

2 Tim 1; 9-10: "This grace was given us in Christ Jesus before the beginning of time, but it has now been revealed through the appearing of our Savior, Christ Jesus, who has destroyed death and has brought life and immortality to light through the gospel." NIV

Rom 8; 28: "And we know that in all things God works for the good of those who love Him, who have been called according to his purpose. For those God Foreknew He also Predestined to be conformed to the likeness of His Son, that He might be the firstborn among many brothers. And those He Predestined He also Called, those He Called, He also Justified, those He Justified, He also Glorified. What then shall we say in response to all of this? God is for us, who can be against us? He (the Father) who did not spare His own Son (Jesus), but gave Him (Jesus) up for us all, how will He (the Father) not also, along with Him (Jesus), graciously give us all things?" NIV

Eph 1;3: "Praise be to the God and Father of our Lord Jesus Christ, who has blessed us in the heavenly realms with every spiritual blessing in Christ. For He chose us in Him before the creation of the world to be holy and blameless in His sight. In love He Predestined us to be adopted as sons through Jesus Christ, in accordance with his pleasure and will, to be the praise of His glorious grace, which He has freely given us in the One He loves. In Him, we have redemption through His blood, the forgiveness of sins, in accordance with the riches of God's grace that He lavished on us with all wisdom and understanding. And He made known to us the mystery of His will according to His good pleasure, which He purposed in Christ, to be put into effect when the times have reached their fulfillment, to bring all things in heaven and on earth together under one head, even Christ.

In Him we were also chosen, having been Predestined according to the pla of Him who works out everything in conformity with the purpose of His will, in order that we, who were the first to hope in Christ, might be for the praise of His glory. And you also were included in Christ when you heard the word of truth, the Gospel of your Salvation. Having believed, you were marked in Him with a seal, the promised Holy Spirit, who is a deposit guaranteeing our inheritance until the redemption of those who are God's possession, to the praise of His glory." NIV

John 3;3: "I tell you the truth no one can see the Kingdom of God unles he is born again. NIV

In the first part of the 'Salvation Enterprise,' the 'Gospel' is the sovereig catalyst for the 'Rebirth' (regeneration) of all who are Foreknown ("before the creation of the world"), Predestined, Called, and Justified. When the Gospe is preached, it sovereignly, by the power of the Holy Spirit, begins a total regeneration of the person who has been 'Called.' In the miracle of rebirth, God destroys the idol of self that had formerly occupied the sinner's Holy of Holies and replaces it with the seal of the Holy Spirit.

In this rebirth, the 'called' sinner is transformed and "blessed in the heavenly realms with every spiritual blessing in Christ." These blessings includ but are not limited to, the following: Godly sorrow for our sins, the ability to Repent of our sins, a God-given Faith to believe in Jesus, Hope, Love, Perseverance, and Joy. These spiritual blessings can be distinguished in character but never separated in essence as they all flow from the Spirit of God into the new believer's life. From that point on, sin no longer reigns (is th boss) in the new believer's life. The believer's task then is to clean out the mar rooms in their temple where the residue of sin remains.

Salvation; Subjective
Human Volition

2nd Cor 7;10-11: "Godly sorrow brings repentance that leads to Salvation and leaves no regret. But worldly sorrow brings death. See what this godly sorrow has produced in you: what earnestness, what eagerness to clear yourselves, what indignation, what alarm, what longing, what concern, what readiness to see justice done." NIV

Rom 10:8: "The word is near you; it is in your mouth and in your heart, that is the word of faith we are proclaiming; That if you confess with your mouth, Jesus is Lord, and believe in your heart that God raised Him from the dead, you will be saved. For it is with your heart that you believe and are justified, and it is with your mouth that you confess and are saved." NIV

In the second aspect of Salvation, the believer responds to God's initial call by calling out to God. This role of human volition follows and yet is wholly dependent upon God's primary sovereign call. The first two gifts of regeneration, Godly sorrow for our sins and the ability to repent of our sins, are essential in leading the newly reborn person to take hold of this newly implanted God-given faith to truly believe.

This call has two parts; professing belief in Jesus as one's Savior from sin and confessing with one's mouth that "Jesus is Lord." "For it is with the heart you that you believe and are justified (forgiveness of sins) and with your mouth that you confess (Lordship) and are saved (eternal life)." God's call begins rebirth, and then the person's answering call complements that eternal moment. The end result of the believer's willful call is that the believer surrenders their will to the will of Jesus and surrenders their life, gaining eternal life in Jesus.

<u>Salvation; Objective;</u>
<u>Water Baptism</u>

By the sixteenth century, the Catholic Church had elevated objective sacramental ceremonies to such an extent that they were considered by the faithful to be God's only and full pathway to Salvation. This legalistic religious structure, called sacerdotalism, was administered exclusively by the priesthood. The subjective requirement of true faith in God at the core of Christ's teaching had been relegated to obscurity.

Due to this sacerdotalism, when the Protestant Reformation came in like a flood, they, in many ways, relegated the sacraments to obscurity. As the second wave of the Protestant Reformation gained full steam, it trivialized anything that remotely resembled Catholicism, including Water Baptism, the Eucharist, Marriage, the lives of the saints, the creeds, and the entire history of the Christian Church between the Apostolic Age and 1517.

Mat 4; 13: "Then Jesus came from Galilee to the Jordan to be baptized by John. But John tried to deter him, saying, "I need to be baptized by you, and do you come to me?" Jesus replied, "Let it be so now, it is proper for us to do this to fulfill all righteousness." Then John consented. As soon as Jesus was baptized, he went up out of the water. At that moment, heaven was opened, and he saw the Spirit of God descending like a dove and lighting on him. And a voice from heaven said, "This is my Son, whom I love, with him I am well pleased." NIV

Mat 28; 19: "Therefore go and make disciples of all nations, baptizing them in the name of the Father and the Son and the Holy Spirit." NIV

Acts 2;38 "Peter replied, "Repent and be baptized, every one of you, in the name of Jesus Christ for the forgiveness of your sins. And you will receive the gift of the Holy Spirit. NIV

Acts 8;36: "As they traveled along the road, they came to some water, and the eunuch said, "Look, here is water. Why shouldn't I be baptized?" NIV

Acts 10;47: "Can anyone keep these people from being baptized with water. They have received the Holy Spirit just as we have. So, he ordered that they be baptized in the name of Jesus Christ." NIV

1 Peter;3;20: "In it (the Ark) only a few people, eight in all, were saved through water, and this water symbolizes baptism that now saves you also - not the removal of dirt from the body but the pledge of a good conscience toward God. It (baptism) saves you by the resurrection of Jesus Christ who has gone into heaven and is at God's right hand – with angels, authorities and powers in submission to Him." NIV

John 3;3: "I tell you the truth no one can see the Kingdom of God unless he is born again....... I tell you the truth, no one can enter the Kingdom of God unless he is born of water and the Spirit. Flesh gives birth to flesh, but Spirit gives birth to Spirit." NIV

Mark 16:16: "Whoever believes and is baptized will be saved" NIV

Nicene Creed; 'One baptism for the forgiveness of sins.'

John the Baptist is considered by most scholars to be the last prophet of the Old Testament who came in the Spirit of Elisia to prepare the way of the coming Messiah. Gentile converts to Judaism in the Old Testament time period were required to undergo a ritual water baptism for cleansing before being accepted into Judaism. John converted this ritual into the Baptism for the Forgiveness of Sins under the Old Law of Sin and Death. However, John knew that he was a sinful man and that his cousin Jesus was the Messiah and, therefore, without sin. That is why he said truthfully, "*I need to be baptized by you.*" The reply of Jesus, "*Let it be so now, it is proper for us to do this to fulfill all righteousness,*" is monumental because one of the major dimensions of "all righteousness" includes the righteousness earned by Jesus on the cross and imputed to the chosen at Salvation.

The third (objective) aspect of Salvation, Water Baptism, completes the miracle of God's redemptive work. When Jesus rose from the waters of the

Jordan River during his Baptism by John, the Trinity was present: Jesus in the material, the Holy Spirit in the likeness of a dove, and the Father vocally. This miracle of the Trinity transformed John's Baptism of Repentance into the Sacrament of Baptism. Christ and the apostles equated Baptism as an integral part of Salvation. In Water Baptism, there is a beautiful physical picture of the spiritual realities of Salvation. The water represents the spiritual cleansing of the Holy Spirit. The emersion below the surface of the water represents the death of Christ. Rising from the water symbolizes Christ's Resurrection. The joining of the redeemed person's body, mind, and spirit, along with the power of the Holy Spirit (in the Sacrament of Water Baptism) cements all three aspects of Salvation into a permanent, eternal covenant between the individual and God.

At this juncture, it is necessary to state emphatically that no ceremony devoid of that person's prior rebirth in Christ and surrender to the Lordship of Christ can gain that person entry into the Kingdom of God. As Jesus said to Nicodemus, a person must be born again of the water and the Spirit. Many believing women experience profound inner healing upon receiving the Sacrament of Water Baptism.

As women are predisposed to a majority Limbic system (emotive) drive, they many times have serious emotional woundings from their time in the world before Salvation. Baptism heals those emotional scars and lets the fountain of the Joy of the Lord begin to spring up in their lives.

Sanctification

We are saved (the event of Salvation), we are being saved (the process of Sanctification), and we will be saved (future Glorification). The eternal moment of 'Salvation' is followed by the lifelong process of dying to self and becoming more like Christ. "Deny yourself, pick up your cross daily, and follow esus (down the Via Dolorosa) is Christ's call to holiness. After the Holy Spirit takes possession of the new believers' Holy of Holies' (in the center of their temple), the lifelong process of cleaning out the rooms in that temple begins. This process involves bringing down out of the believer's eternal bank account, in the heavenly realms, every spiritual blessing in Christ. Then, the believer's task is to make these giftings real and effective in a woefully fallen world. This process is essential to sustain Christian growth.

Heb 12; 14: "Without holiness, no one will see God." NIV

Glorification

When we die and enter into the Kingdom of God, the eternal process of reflecting the Glory of God in heaven begins.

The Eucharist

John 6; 53: "Jesus said to them, "I tell you the truth, unless you eat the flesh of the Son of Man and drink His blood, you have no life in you. Whoever eats my flesh and drinks my blood has eternal life, and I will raise him up on the last day." NIV

Luke 22;19: And He took bread, gave thanks and broke it, and gave it to them, saying "This is my body given for you do this in remembrance of me." In the same way, after the supper, he took the cup, saying, "This cup is the new covenant in my blood, which is poured out for you." NIV

1 Cor 11; 27: "Therefore, whoever eats the bread or drinks the cup of the Lord in an unworthy manner will be guilty of sinning against the body and blood of the Lord. A man ought to examine himself before he eats the bread and drinks the cup. For anyone who eats and drinks without recognizing the body of the Lord eats and drinks judgement on himself. That is why many among you are weak and sick, and a number of you have fallen asleep (died).

But if we judged ourselves, we would not come under judgement. When we ar *judged by the Lord, we are being disciplined so that we will not be condemned* *by the world."* NIV

The Jewish Passover came about during the last days of Israel's captivity in Egypt. The tenth and last plague God brought upon Egypt, through the agency of Moses, was the slaughter of all the firstborn males in Egypt. In protecting the Israelites from this plague, God ordered Moses to instruct t people to take a lamb without blemish, slaughter it, and sprinkle its blood on th doorposts and the lintels of their houses. (A Lintel is the beam that rests on top of the doorposts supporting the structures above the door.) The blood c the lamb caused the Angel of Death to pass-over the houses of the Israelites thereby sparing their firstborn males.

Thereafter, the Passover became a yearly celebration of the Salvation from death of the firstborn Israelite male by the blood of the lamb. The Passover also celebrates the subsequent freedom of the Israelite people from slavery in Egypt. In the celebration of the Last Supper, Jesus transformed the Passover into the Sacrament of the Holy Eucharist, whereby believers celebrate their freedom from the slavery and death caused by sin.

Luther believed that the bread and wine did not physically change but tha Jesus physically entered both elements. This can be visualized in the analogy of a sponge soaking up water. Calvin, on the other hand, did not believe that Christ was physically present in the elements. Calvin taught that believers ar spiritually raised up to Christ in heaven due to the Eucharist. During a meeting between Luther and Calvin, a very heated argument arose between t two men on this issue. In this maelstrom, Luther could be heard yelling full for at Calvin in Latin, "What part of "This is my body" do you not understand." Many theological views of 'Holy Communion' persist to the present. Howev the undeniable truth is that it is Holy unto God. The Greek Orthodox

Church does not try to logically explain the Eucharist but simply calls the Communion a Sacred Mystery.

The Roman Catholic Church established the doctrine of Transubstantiation in 1215 at the Fourth Council of Lateran. The Roman Church, utilizing Aristotle's definition of substance, determined that the material and formal aspects of the substances of bread and wine were transformed physically into the true body and true blood of Christ. The Roman Church further stated that only the external properties, 'the Accidens,' remained in the appearance and texture of bread and wine.

The actual ceremonial ritual of the Sacrament of the Eucharist, as practiced by the Roman Catholic Church, had become the principal focus of the laity. This physical ritual was, to most Catholics, in and of itself, the sole instrument of Sanctification. The Power of the Holy Spirit was thus trivialized in the sacrament.

Due to the Catholic focus on ritual, many second-generation Protestant Churches viewed the Catholic Eucharist as a form of religious idolatry. In a majority of present-day Protestant Churches, Communion has been reduced to a mere 'remembrance.' Many Protestant Churches now utilize a cheap machine stamped out, plastic enclosure that contains colored sugar water and a wafer. The congregants nonchalantly ingest the elements, and the package is then discarded into the rubbish. This form of very superficial communion begs the question, is this blatant trivialization of the sacred "an unworthy manner?"

In consideration of what the Catholic Eucharist had become by the start of the sixteenth century, a physical examination of the 'Holy Grail' can be seen as a very useful analogy. The Cathedral of Valencia in Spain houses what is traditionally believed to be the 'Holy Grail' itself, i.e., the cup used by Jesus to celebrate the Last Supper.

In its current form, the storied "Holy Chalice of Valencia" consists of two parts. The simple upper and interior cup is regarded as the original cup of

Jesus. This cup is made of red agate stone, semi-spherical in shape, sometimes described as the size of an orange cut in half. The outer surrounding part of the chalice is adorned with gold, pearls, rubies, and emeralds and rests on an elaborate stem. This exterior part of the chalice is considered a medieval addition.

The simple cup at the center (whether it is the original article or not) represents the cup of an itinerate Rabi of the early first century who had no material possessions other than the clothes on His back. With simple bread and ordinary wine, He, by the power of the Holy Spirit, transformed them gloriously into His spiritual flesh and His spiritual blood. The external part of the chalice represents the material trappings that man, in his vanity, has added to this amazing miracle.

In an even deeper understanding, the entire material structure of this chalice is only a mere relic at best. It is Jesus and the miracle He established at the Last Supper that allows only a truly regenerated believer to enter into the fullness of Christ. In this miracle, the believer's spiritual body is refreshed by Christ's spiritual body and his soul is cleansed of the effects of sin by the spiritual blood of Jesus.

In depression, self-focus has locked the individual into a painfully hopeless mentality that pulls the person ever downward into a vortex of darkness. When a believer struggling with depression receives the Sacred Eucharist, the Holy Spirit shatters the grip of this personal self-focus. Holy Communion reestablishes the believer's physical, mental, and spiritual oneness with Christ. This Holy Sacrament leads to the restoration of their 'First Love' awakening the full joy of their Salvation. The Holy Eucharist thereby heals depression and anxiety, achieving true victory in the believer's life. Women, being twice as afflicted as men with depression, have come to understand that Holy Communion is the heavenly highway to fully restored mental health and well-being.

The Sacrament of Marriage

In His first miracle, Jesus turned water into wine at a wedding feast. This miracle, in the first place, served as an analogy where water (the ordinary) is transformed into wine (the sacred). Secondly, but most importantly, by this miracle, Christ transformed Marriage, the major social event in Jewish culture, into the Sacrament of Marriage.

Martin Luther recognized only two sacraments: Baptism and the Eucharist. By taking Marriage out of the sacramental realm, Luther set the stage for the breakdown and dissolution of the family structure we are currently witnessing in society as a whole. Unredeemed men insist on uncommitted romantic and sexual relationships with women. In this modality, the unregenerate male has everything to gain. Women, on the other hand, very much need commitment in relationships to ensure emotional and material security. The Sacrament of Marriage is holy because it represents the Marriage of Jesus with his "Bride," the true church of the living God.

However, simply going through a ceremony does not transform the ordinary into the sacred. It takes a truly regenerated woman and a truly regenerated man vouchsafing oneness in body, mind, and spirit, by the power of the Holy Spirit, for the Sacrament of Marriage to be genuine. In the Sacrament of Marriage, the lives of both parties are welded together, forming a life-long bond that holds both the couple and the family they create together in a storm-tossed world.

Mary, Mother of Jesus.

The Catholic Church was declared to be the official religion of the Roman Empire in 321 AD by Emperor Constantine. After that event, the

Church slowly began to fall into the process of institutionalization. The Church at Rome caved into the Roman culture of the day by placing statues of Jesus, Mary, and the Saints in the Roman Catholic churches. This was in direct disobedience of the second commandment.

Ex 20: *Thou shalt not make for yourself any graven image, or any likeness of anything in heaven above or on the earth beneath or in the waters below. Thou shalt not bow down to them or worship them.* NIV

The hierarchy of the Roman Church made the formal distinction that the statues were there only to remind the faithful of the Saints. However, the laity were not mindful of this nuance and quickly fell into idolatry of the statues themselves. The Roman Catholic Hierarchy saw this idolatry and, in point of fact, encouraged it.

Due to this idolatry, there had been a long history of a 'Mary Cult' within the Roman Catholic Church. This cult held that Mary was conceived without sin (Immaculate Conception). Mary was thereby elevated, by this cult, to the status of co-redeemer with Christ. In the 'Mary Cult' this co-redeemer designation made Mary (a created being) equal with Jesus (the creator). As a very late development in the history of the Roman Catholic Church, Pope Pius IX established the 'Immaculate Conception' as De Fedi (must believe) doctrine in a Papal Bulla.

Then, Pius IX etched it in stone with the establishment of the 'Impermatter Excathedra' doctrine. The 'Impermatter Excathedra' doctrine declared that when the Pope spoke on issues of doctrine or morality, he was infallible. This errant assumption of inerrancy by Pope Pius IX was the beginning of what has been labeled 'The Imperial Papacy.'

However, the 'Immaculate Conception of Mary' concept had been debunked down through the centuries by the major theologians within the Catholic Church. The theologians St Augustine, St. Thomas Aquinas, S Barnard, St Anselm, Albert the Great, Bonaventure, and Peter Lombard a

jected the argument that Mary was conceived without sin. They only
sputed as to when, after her conception, Mary became sinless.

Mary was conceived by the physical union of her father and her mother,
nna. Mary, a created being, although highly exalted among humans, was
measurably below God in status. Therefore, Mary was born into original
n. However, Mary had to be perfectly holy herself in order to conceive and
ve birth to the perfectly holy God/Man. At Salvation, both 'Original Sin'
d the stain of 'Original Sin' were cleansed from Mary's person and spirit.
lary is unique in that she was entirely sanctified at the moment of her spiritual
birth.

The Protestant Church, in order to eliminate worship and prayer to
ary, relegated Mary to a non-person status only to be superficially
entioned in passing at Christmas. It can be reasonably argued that this
asting aside' by the Protestant Church went too far to the opposite pole. So,
nat then, is the balance point in a truly biblical theology of Mary?

Mary was not only the mother of Jesus; Mary was the person God used
bring the human part of Jesus into full maturity. Mary was uniquely designed
God to bring up Jesus in the nurture and admonition of the Lord. The
man portion of Jesus had to be trained from birth in all of the necessary
quirements of life.

Immersion in the loving personality of Mary's gifted mind and spirit made
arning fun and enjoyable for the young child Jesus. Mary taught Jesus to
ad utilizing the Old Testament Scriptures. Mary lovingly conveyed the
iritual truth of scripture along with its life application. Mary instilled God's
ith through her words and by her actions throughout the course of every day.
ary modeled the reality of scripture in everything she did, from her cleaning of
e house, to her sewing of garments, to her purchasing of food in the
arketplace, to her preparing meals for the family.

Mary serves as the ultimate role model for women. Mary, in presenting th
baby Jesus in the temple for the 'Consecration of the firstborn' was told by t
prophet Simion,

Luke 2;35: "and a sword will pierce your own soul too." NIV

Those God uses greatly, He first wounds greatly. Mary's life of pain
and sorrow, then victory, serves as an inspiration for all women. Mary
demonstrated how to daily walk out an ever more godly life in an increasingly e
world.

If, by the grace of God, you were miraculously afforded the opportunity
to sit down alone at a quiet table with Mary, what would be your experience?
The gravity of her presence would draw you with a soft tenderness like an
unweaned fawn to its doe. The warmth of her radiant smile would melt away al
your secret apprehensions. Her joyful eyes would sparkle like a sunrise on
newly fallen snow to fully illuminate all the shadowed corners of your heart.
Her voice, enrapturing as a clear mountain spring rippling its symphony over
rounded stones, would grace your ears. Then perhaps Mary would say
something on the order of the following: "Please, my dear friend, do not worsh
me; I am a fellow servant just like you; worship my glorious son Jesus, the Lord
of the Entire Universe. In Him and Him alone resides eternal life. An eterna
life full of innocent purity and endless joyous adoration of the Ancient of
Days."

Mary Magdalene

Mary Magdalene was a disciple of Jesus who struggled with sin before
she came to know Jesus.

Luke 8:2: "Mary, called Magdalene, from whom seven demons had com
out." NIV

Pope Gregory the Great ascertained that Mary Magdalene was the
woman in:

Luke 7:37; "When a woman who had lived a sinful life in that town learned that Jesus was eating at the Pharisee's house, she brought an alabaster jar of perfume, and as she knelt behind him at his feet weeping, she began to wet his feet with her tears. Then she wiped them with her hair, kissed them, and poured perfume on them." NIV

Luke 7:47: "Therefore I tell you, her many sins have been forgiven, for she loved much. Then Jesus said to her your sins are forgiven." NIV

Mary Magdalene was the first to see the resurrected Jesus;

John 20;1: "Early on the first day of the week, while it was still dark, Mary Magdalene went to the tomb and saw that the stone had been removed from the entrance....Mary stood outside the tomb crying. As she wept, she bent over to look into the tomb and saw two angels in white, seated where Jesus' body had been, one at the head and the other at the foot. They asked her, "Woman, why are you crying?" "They have taken my Lord away," she said, "and I don't know where they have put him." At this, she turned around and saw Jesus standing there, but she did not realize that it was Jesus. "Woman," he said, "why are you crying? Who is it that you are looking for?" Thinking he was the gardener, she said, "If you have carried him away, tell me where you have put him, and I will get him." Jesus said to her, "Mary." She turned toward him and cried out in Aramaic, "Rabboni!" (which means teacher) Jesus said, "Do not hold on to me, for I have not yet returned to the Father. Go instead to my brothers and tell them, I am returning to my Father and your Father, to my God and your God." NIV

Legend has it that, sometime after the ascension of Jesus, during a time of persecution, Mary Magdalene was exiled from Israel. The Legend relates that Mary Magdalene, Lazarus, Mary Salome, Mary Jacobe, Maximin, and their Egyptian servant Sara were forced into a boat without sail or rudder and set adrift on the Mediterranean Sea. The ship was guided by the hand of God to Provence of Gaul. Upon landing in Provence, some of the group remained there while others set off to preach the gospel. The men headed east, where Lazarus became the first bishop of Marseille and Maximin became the first bishop of Aix-en-Provence.

Mary Magdalene traveled with Lazarus, where she stayed for some time in Marseille, spreading the gospel. At some point, Mary Magdalene continued her journey into the mountainous region of Gaul and settled in a large cave in the mountains that served as a grotto. After spending three decades in prayer and devotion to God in her mountain grotto, she traveled to Aix-en-Provence. Upon arriving in Aix-en-Provence, she received communion from her old friend Maximin and died shortly thereafter.

Two Maries

Two women, both named Mary, both chosen by God. One Mary had led a life of piety and obedience; the other Mary had lived a life of sin and degradation. Both Maries needed a Savior; both had surrendered their lives to God and were reborn. Both Maries had watched Jesus, their Messiah, already scourged almost to death, shoulder his splintered wooden cross beam, and walk the Via Dolorosa. Both Maries stood in an emotional free fall on the hill at Golgotha as Jesus was nailed to the cross. Both Maries watched their Lord and Savior writhing in utter agony as He died on that cross.

At noon, darkness descended upon Jerusalem as the sun lost its light. At mid-afternoon, Jesus called out in a loud voice, "It is finished, Father, into your hands I commit my spirit," Then Jesus breathed His last. Both Maries, along with ten thousand times ten thousand angels who were gathered at Golgotha, wept a river of holy tears. Both Maries were selected by God to share in the sufferings of Christ. Both Maries exhibited the strength, the compassion, and the love of the Father at an elevated level that only women are gifted by God to exert.

Wonderous Woman

In Christianity complete surrender of a person's will to the will of the Living God is the door of entry into eternal life! Christianity, not being of this world, a relationship with the Living God that is supported by cogent religious precepts. Therefore, the priorities of this material world; wealth, power, and strength, are set aside for the priorities of God; Faith, Hope, and Love. God's noblest creation, Woman, is a living manifestation of these eternal virtues of which Love is the highest.

God, the perfect engineer, designed women to perfectly complete the ighest material purpose of human existence: to bring forth and nurture human life. Due to this life-bringer role, God's superior design of women gave them exponentially expanded genetic expression. Therefore, He made them vastly superior to men in all the elements that make life more beautiful, profoundly meaningful, and joyfully worth living.

It is fitting at this juncture to return to an exploration of God's order of creation. God created the world from the least to the greatest with an ever-increasing complexity and beauty. God first created the heavens immense and expansive beyond all description. Call to mind a moonless night in your childhood when you first gazed in wonder at the amazing spectacle of the Milky Way.

And God saw that it was good. NIV

Then, God created the vibrant earth. Think of all the beauty of a spring sunrise standing on a mountainside overlooking a beautiful valley full of tall fir trees and lush vegetation.

And God saw that it was good. NIV

Yet with all this beauty God saw that creation was not complete. Therefore, God created all the incredible animals. Put yourself on a boat floating on the vast blue Pacific Ocean; suddenly, a sailfish breaks the surface of the deep, coming entirely out of the water. Your mind captures its glorious splendor at the height of its arc. Consider a wild mare running at full gallop, with its mane and tail in the wind. The wild horse certainly must be one of the most magnificent of God's creatures.

And God saw that it was good. N/V

Creation being incomplete at this juncture, God created man in His very image and likeness. Still, God was not finished! After creating man, God saw the need to go one step better. He then created Woman, more complex and much more beautiful than all of the rest of His creation.

God saw all that He had made, and it was very good. N/V

Woman's beauty is not merely superficial in its manifestation. This overwhelming symphony of excellent light is profound and captivating because originates from the fountains of the 'Water of Life' surging from deep within the female soul. This beauty is exalted in the marvelous good deeds she performs for those all around her in a myriad of ways. Her gentle teaching of the young on how to live joyfully in the presence of the eternal God. Her caring for the elderly giving them value when they feel so devalued by an uncaring world. Her watering the spiritual gardens of those who struggle with the abject vacant emptiness of depression. Her giving to the destitute who have so very little in today's world of opulent materialism. These acts of tender kindness flow out the overwhelming empathy abundantly gifted to women by a loving God.

Wonderous Woman, the bringer of life and the pinnacle of created Love reigns generously as the Glorious Crown of God's Marvelous Creation.

Sources

) John Innes Centre, Proof Mendel discovered the laws of inheritance decades ahead of
s time. 2022, ScienceDaily and other Internet Sources.

) Dijk, Ellis, et al., Mendel Discoveries, Nature Genetics, 2022, ScienceDaily and other
ternet Sources.

) Byrne et al., Nettie Stephens; Female research pioneer, 2018, ScienceDaily and other
ternet Sources.

) Breast Cancer, Cleveland Clinic online, Mayo Clinic online, CDC online, ACS
line, NCI online, WHO online. and other Internet Sources.

) Migeon et al., X Inactivation, JAMA, 2006 and other Internet Sources.

) Deng et al.; Nature Genetics 2011, and other Internet Sources.

) Carrel et al., Penn State; Men and Women: Differences are in the Genes: Penn State.
005. ScienceDaily and other Internet Sources.

) Russo, Gault et al., Molecular Biology and Evolution; Oxford University Press, 2013.
cienceDaily and other Internet Sources.

) Willard, Vilain, Visootsak, et al., MedlinePlus; X Chromosome, 2005

0) Mitchell, McLanahan, et al., Father Loss and Child Telomere Length. Pediatrics,
17.

1) Friedrich Miescher, NIH online, Princeton University online and other Internet
ources.

2) DNA from the beginning: Pheobus Lavene, 2002, dnaftb.org and other Internet
ources.

3) DNA Learning Center: Pheobus Lavene, cshl.edu and other Internet Sources.

4) Kresge, Simoni, Hill, et al., Chargaff's Rules: Journal of Biological Chemistry, 2005.

5) Cohen, Lehman, et al., Erwin Chargaff: NAS online, 2010.

6) Scientific Women; Rosalind Franklin, Wikipedia and other Internet Sources.

7) Rosalind Franklin: DNA, Facts, and Death. Biography.com

8) Franklin, Crick, Watson, Science History Institute, 2022, and other Internet Sources.

9) Elaine N Marieb, Human Anatomy and Physiology 2nd Ed, 1992   Without a
oubt, The Best Anatomy and Physiology Textbook Ever Published.

0) Ovarian Cancer: CDC online, Mayo Clinic online, ACS online, NCI online, and
er Internet Sources.

) Are Women more Empathtic: Oxford Academic online,

(22) Women's Empathy: NIH online, Pew Research Center online, and other Internet Sources.

(23) Christov, Moore, et al., Empathy: Gender effects in brain and behavior, 2014.

(24) Loffler et al., Women the more empathetic Gender, 2023.

(25) Women's Depression: ADAA online, MHA online, CDC online, NIMH online, and other Internet Sources.

(26) Lasiuk et al., Hormone Fluctuations / Mood Disturbances In Women, Univ Alberta 2007, ScienceDaily.

(27) Elsevier, Men and Women have opposite genetic alterations in Depression, 2018, ScienceDaily.

(28) Women's Depression: Mind Brain: ScienceDaily; Various Research Abstracts.

(29) Anwar et al., As Married Couples Age, UCB. 2018. ScienceDaily.

(30) Oravecz, Dirsmith, et al., Experiencing Love in Everyday Life, Penn State. 2020. ScienceDaily.

(31) Bakker, Boehm, et al, Kisspeptin: Brain Controls Sex, Saarland Univ 2018. ScienceDaily.

(32) Demas, Kriegsfeld, et al, Kisspeptin Levels, Indiana Univ. 2006. ScienceDaily.

(33) Human Romantic Love; Harvard Med School online, PT online, APA online, BB SFM online, UOW online, and other Internet Sources.

(34) Human Romantic Love: Mind Brain: ScienceDaily; Various Research Abstracts.

(35) Acevedo, Poulin, Brown. Beyond Romance: Empathy and Bonding. USCSB, 2019 ScienceDaily.

(36) Chimera: Mothers Brain: Robert Martone, mind brain/science daily

(37) The New Science of Motherhood: Smithsonian Magazine, Chaudry

(38) Chimera: Healthline, NIH, SD, SA, and other Internet Sources.

(39) Male Aggression: Mind Brain: ScienceDaily; Various Research Abstracts.

(40) Female Elementary School Teachers: Pew Research Centers, Mind Brain: ScienceDaily Various Research Abstracts.

(41) Feminization of teaching in America: MIT

(42) Women in K-12 Workforce: Education Week

(43) Genetic explanation for cancer's higher incidence in males than females: Dana-Farber Cancer Institute.

(44) The Grieving Heart; Bob Dorsett

(45) Takotsubo Syndrome; BHF, Mayo Clinic, St Vincents HH, and other Internet Sources.

(46) Pesticide Side Effects: NH, IFM, Frontiers, ScienceDirect, and other Internet Sources.

(47) Alcoholism: Mayo Clinic, NIAAA, CDC, Medscape, and other Internet Sources.

(48) Divorce: Psychology Today, AJP, Gottman Institute, Research Gate, and other Internet Sources.

(49) Progressive Supranuclear Palsy: Johns Hopkins Medicine, Mayo Clinic, Cleveland Clinic, and other Internet Sources.

(50) Visual Cortex: Mind Brain: ScienceDaily; Various Research Abstracts.

(51) Keysers, Gazzole, et al., Brain Expectation, Netherlands IN, 2023, ScienceDaily and other Internet Sources.

Made in the USA
Monee, IL
22 September 2024

65685566R00069